Whiskey & Water

Vaela Quinn

Tess Daley Publishing

Dedication

For my husband—thank you for believing in me from the very beginning, for surviving the all-nighters, and for never questioning that I'd finish what I started.

For Alice, whose relentless insistence kept me honest and moving forward when stopping would have been easier.

And for Natalie and Vicki—your thoughtful, generous feedback helped Sloane and Daniel step fully into the light. This story is stronger because of you.

Contents

Chapter 1

D aniel sees her nearly every Tuesday—the only night he pretends to relax. Off the clock, in town, not out somewhere surviving whatever off-the-books job landed in his lap.

Not because the place is special, but because in a small town it's a second living space—a weathered bar where restless heels have polished the brass rail for decades and the jukebox still believes Fleetwood Mac can fix almost anything.

Two mahogany stools separate them. One holds her jacket; the other an empty space like a proper chaperone.

The air tastes like rosemary fries and old bourbon, salt and smoke soaked into wood. The stained-glass exit sign glows with borrowed light, washing the doorway in shifting color. Conversations rise and fall around them—small tides of laughter and low arguments. Somewhere behind her, Stevie Nicks promises she'll never break the chain.

Sloane winds her silver chain around her fingers, leather boots perched on the footrail's patina, marking time without thinking. Daniel's fountain pen moves in slow, deliberate strokes. His Irish coffee waits at his elbow — a drink a man savors, not rushes—as his gaze sweeps the exits and corners out of practiced habit.

Daniel had been sketching notes for a new lyric when the sound of silver against glass cut through the jukebox hum. He glanced sideways.

The woman two stools down reached for her drink, swirled it, watching the amber shift. She took a sip, then set it down. Looking at her left hand, she removed a thin silver band along with a thicker, loose-fitting band beneath. Placing them into the velvet pouch, she tucked both the rings and the pouch back into her front right pocket.

"Sam—prickly pear. Half salt."

Sam didn't look at her first—his gaze lifted to the *If You Were Born On This Date, You're 21 Today* calendar Rosemary's used as a cheap stand-in for a clock.

A breath left him, slow and measured. He nodded once and reached for the tequila.

"You'll hate the taste," the bartender muttered.

She smiled, small and crooked. "Always did."

Daniel closed his notebook. Whatever line he'd been chasing tonight didn't matter anymore.

Sam set the glass down—rose-pink, rim half-crusted with salt. A gummy worm clung to the skewer, stabbed through the middle like it was trying to crawl its way out. The bartender even touched her hand—brief, respectful.

"Here, luv," Sam said quietly. "We all miss him, but we don't know the weight you carry. You sit, take as long as you need. And if you need longer, that's why—"

Her palm pressed to his, finishing with him in unison: "—the Universe gives us friends."

Daniel's hand stilled on his Irish coffee. The familiarity between them was unmistakable—affection worn smooth, the kind that only came from words said too many times to count.

She took a long pull from the glass and winced. "Gods. Still tastes like a sour gummy worm took a tequila bath."

Sam laughed, easy, like he'd heard it a hundred times. He set a water down in front of her. "Did it taste like what you expected?"

"Yeah," she said, voice steadier. She pushed the salted glass aside.

Daniel sipped his Irish coffee and set it back down, attention fixed on her.

***

Daniel had seen her here before. Every Tuesday he managed to make it to Rosemary's—often enough in the past ten months to learn her rhythm. Always whiskey. Neat. Sometimes she talked. Sometimes she sat quiet with the chain looped around her fingers. Always steady.

Tonight broke pattern.

The rings. The Prickly Pear. The laugh with rust in it.

He didn't get up. Not yet. Just tipped his chair back enough for his voice to carry low across the two stools between them.

"Didn't know that was ever on the board," he said. His eyes flicked to the half salted glass Sam had set aside.

Sam shot him a look—careful, warning. But the woman didn't flinch.

She turned her head slowly, studying him like she was deciding whether he was a shadow she'd clocked before or someone worth acknowledging now.

Daniel met her gaze. Steady.

She lifted the whiskey instead, the glass cool and familiar in her hand, turned it once before answering.

"Mac was tough as hell," she said. Rougher now. Real. "He would've clocked you ten months ago—the first night you walked in. Man didn't miss much."

A beat.

"Always joked the sweet, sour, salty kick—and the prickly name—were practice for the day he met me. "A smile crossed her eyes. "The garnish was my fault. Sam added it later."

Something shifted low in Daniel's gut.

The second ring. The bartender's care. The way this drink wasn't ordered so much as *remembered*.

He let the silence sit long enough for the jukebox to swallow her words, then leaned forward, forearms on the bar.

"Sounds like a man who didn't waste excuses," he said. His eyes flicked—from the glass in her hand to the velvet pouch tucked into her pocket. "Prickly or not."

***

She tilted her head, studying him, the chain coiled tight around her fingers again. "You always analyze people's drink orders, or is this special treatment?"

"Just yours. "Just the fact of it, laid out in his quiet voice.

Sam's brows jumped like he might interfere, but Sloane waved him off with a flick of her hand — small, sharp, practiced.

"You've been watching me. "Not a question.

Daniel tapped the closed notebook once, then slid it farther from him. "I notice things," he said. "And you've made yourself hard to miss."

For the first time that night, her mouth curved. A crooked, knowing little pull — a look that told him she'd clocked him.

"Mac would've hated and respected you for that."

Daniel held her gaze. "He seemed like a good man."

Her smile shifted, edges softening. "He was."

She nodded toward the notebook. "A year might seem long to some, but not to others. The soul processes at its own pace." Her eyes narrowed, sharpening again. "You don't look like a writer. Or a cop. So... private security? Or just old-school enough to prefer ink over screens?"

A breath left him — almost a laugh, but not quite. He turned the notebook a fraction with one finger, pulling it closer.

"Not a writer," he said. "Not a cop. And I own a phone." His voice dipped. "I just prefer the intimacy of pen and paper."

Her hand hovered near the notebook. "So what do you actually put in there? Drawings? Lines? Surveillance notes?"

"Lyrics," he said. "Fragments. Inspiration when it shows up. Just... things that quiet the noise. Journaling never stuck."

Her head tilted, the chain loosening between her fingers. "That's military or cop talk if I've ever heard it."

Daniel felt the corner of his mouth lift — brief, controlled. "Or maybe it's just me admitting I watch more than I talk."

She nudged the notebook back toward him with a knuckle. "Nice. I had a diary in high school. Kept it tucked under the middle of my parents' mattress. Brilliant idea until I checked under the bed on a very unfortunate day."

She grimaced, half horrified, half amused. "At that age we still want to believe storks bring babies — not that our parents actually have coitus."

She held his gaze while she said it — *coitus*, crisp and deliberate — like she was laying something sharp between them and watching to see if he'd bleed.

Daniel's Irish coffee paused halfway to his mouth. He caught the word choice first. Then the intent beneath it.

"Middle of the mattress," he said, lowering the cup. "Rookie mistake. Always check for hazards before you stash contraband."

Her mouth quirked, but her eyes stayed sharp.

"As for storks—" he leaned in, voice dropping, gravel threading through, "—the world runs out of fairy tales faster than we expect."

The chain stilled between her fingers.

"You were looking for a reaction," he said quietly. "Here it is: you're sharp. Funny." His gaze flicked to her whiskey glass. "And you don't hide the burn when you're ready to feel it."

Something shifted in her gaze.

"You're right," she said. "Pretty window dressing fades fast when you've run calls. Too much shit is real."

She took a long, steady pull from her whiskey, letting the burn root her to the barstool.

Daniel's eyes narrowed. He knew the weight of that phrasing — the way it sat in the throat, the way it carried memories you didn't talk about unless someone else understood.

"Yeah," he said, voice roughened, stripped to truth. "Too real. Too fast."

She tipped her glass again, slower now, like she needed the warmth to stay anchored.

Daniel didn't look away.

"I know that world," he said quietly. "Different patch, same silence before the worst of it lands."

Her hand stilled on the rim of her glass. The chain dangled once, then went still too.

He knew that look.

Knew what it took to stand on the far side of it.

***

For the first time tonight, his gaze wasn't cataloguing or testing—it was just there, solid, weighted with something he knew well.

She nodded. "EMT. Eight years. Quit—last year." She glanced unintentionally at her left hand, now bare. "It's been a year today. Call went out. I was already at a scene. I didn't know, but my heart did, and when I heard it was an 80s Mustang t-boned by a semi, I knew. He drove the only Fox body in town."

Daniel didn't move. Not when her eyes flicked to her bare hand, not when the words dropped like broken glass between them.

He breathed in slowly, steadily, like he was absorbing every fragment she'd just laid out. His hand flexed once against the bar top, the only tell he let slip.

"I didn't hear the call," he corrected softly. "But I felt the silence that followed it. Some things hit a town like a shockwave."

Her gaze snapped back to him, sharp, searching.

Daniel's eyes held steady on hers. "Some weights don't leave when you clock out. Not the scene. Not the man." He tapped his knuckles once against the bar, a quiet punctuation. "And no one else can shoulder what's carved into your bones."

For a moment, the bar noise fell away. Her glass sat between them, untouched, the air heavier with what she'd just laid out.

She took a slow breath. "Therapy wasn't my thing. Found better healing with a Harley vibrating under me and ink needles in my hand." Her fingers tapped a rhythm against her glass. "Almost done with my apprenticeship at Flock of Ink."

Daniel's brow lifted at that—his read of it: therapy with iron between her legs. He recognized survival.

"Flock of Ink," he echoed, the corner of his mouth tugging like he could already picture the needle, the gun, the skin canvas. "So you traded saving bodies for marking them."

She shrugged unapologetically. "Some people heal with scars. Some with pictures of wolves or roses over them."

Daniel let the thought sit. Then, he tipped his chin at her. "Apprenticeship finishes next month. You've got a direction. A lane."

She turned her glass, slow, deliberate. "That was the point." Her eyes cut back to him. "And you?"

Daniel's Irish coffee had long gone cold. He set it aside, both hands resting flat on the bar now. "Contract work. Security. Clean up messes other people can't. I don't stay in one place long."

He studied her a beat longer, voice quieter. "But I come back here."

He'd been respectful. Never saw her with a partner—man or woman. Maybe he'd caught a hint or two over the months, but the rings had been the real boundary.

"I'm Sloane, by the way. Though I'd be disappointed if you hadn't picked that up in ten months, Daniel. Right?"

Daniel's mouth curved—not quite a smile, but enough to register she'd noticed. "Yeah. Daniel."

He let her name sit between them, rolling it once, slow. Sloane. The rings had always drawn the line for him. Months of quiet nods, the occasional glance, nothing more.

"You'd be right," he said finally. "Months of Tuesdays. Hard not to pick up a name when you hear Sam say it every time he slides your glass down the bar."

Sam grunted from the taps, not bothering to deny it.

Sloane's eyes narrowed, playful but sharp. "So you've been listening."

"Respectfully," Daniel countered, voice low, steady. "Boundaries matter. But tonight..." His gaze flicked once, just briefly, to her bare hand, then back to her face. "Tonight you moved the line."

The chain twisted around her fingers again, but her hand didn't tremble. "Maybe I did."

Daniel leaned in just enough for the space between them to tighten. "Absolutely, you did."

Sam muttered something from the taps—something that sounded a whole lot like *finally*. Sloane shot him a look sharp enough to cut glass, heat snapping back into her spine. She knocked once on the bar top decisively. "Sam, I'm leaving my bike here. I'll walk down to the shop—Kerry'll grab it before you close. I've got a client in two hours, large piece to finish sketching."

Then she turned to Daniel, the corner of her mouth lifting. "Next Tuesday then..."

She didn't wait for his answer. She stood tall, grabbed the jacket off the buffer stool Sam always left between her and the customers, and walked out without a backward glance.

Daniel watched her go, the scrape of the stool loud in the silence she left behind. There was no hesitation in her stride.

***

Daniel hit the basement like gravity meant to pin him there. Concrete floor, cold steel, the hum of the old dehumidifier—the closest thing he had to a church. No noise. No eyes. No questions. Just iron, sweat, and the illusion he still controlled something.

His shirt hit the bench. The wraps went around his hands on muscle memory. His body still ran hot from drills and reports, the kind of burn that normally wiped thoughts clean.

Not tonight.

Tonight, all he saw was her.

Tonight she had cracked open—rings slipping into velvet, voice catching around a joke that wasn't a joke, pain showing through the steel.

He grabbed the dumbbells and started a set that should've emptied his head. It didn't touch her.

Her laugh—too sharp, too rusty .Her smile—dangerous, beautiful, the kind that hit like a blade. Her legs long in worn denim, boots scuffed, leather hugging her frame like it knew her better than anyone alive. The ink on her upper arm—a wild mustang tearing free through thorned roses. A woman who wore freedom and pain on the same damn canvas.

He lifted harder. Faster. Let the burn climb.

For ten months he'd kept her on the far side of a line he never crossed. A woman wearing rings wasn't his to want. He was trained to hold boundaries—hell, he survived on them.

But tonight?

Tonight she moved the line. Took off the rings. Did it herself. And he felt that shift like a punch to the ribs.

The weights hit the floor with a thud that shook dust from the rafters. Not enough.

He jumped on the treadmill next—speed high, incline higher. Pound. Pound. Pound.

Her voice echoed with every step:

"Mac was tough as hell.", "He would've clocked you.", "I'm fine."

She wasn't—by his measure. But she was honest. And honesty, coming from a woman built of edges and old scars, hit harder than any workout.

The treadmill whined under the pace he pushed. His lungs burned. His legs screamed. Still not enough.

He killed the machine and stripped the rest of the way down. The cold shower came on full blast, water slamming him like ice.

Didn't stop her. Nothing did.

The image of her—bare hand on the bar where rings used to be, chain slipping through her fingers, grief and fire braided together—followed him under the water.

He braced both palms on the tile, breath rough.

He'd seen people break after loss. Seen grief twist good men into ghosts and good women into stone.

But Sloane? She carried it like a weight she'd welded to herself—too proud to drop, too loyal to cut loose, too exhausted to keep dragging. And tonight she'd set it down. Right there at the bar. In front of him.

When the water finally warmed and his heartbeat loosened its fist around his ribs, he shut it off and toweled down.

Sleep wasn't coming. He knew it. So he dressed—black joggers, a fitted tee—and headed to his office instead.

Paperwork. Schedules. Contracts. All useless tonight.

Eventually he opened the rotation calendar and dragged his name off Wednesday.

Next week was too damn far away.

By the time exhaustion finally pulled him under, hours before dawn, one thought settled in with the weight of a decision already made:

Tomorrow, Sloane Calder, I move my boundaries too.

***

Sloane pulled the velvet pouch from her pocket, rubbing her thumb along the soft seam as she walked down the narrow hall. The overhead light cast a warm glow on the familiar creaks beneath her feet, each one sounding like the house exhaling with her. She moved straight toward the bedroom, toward the small wooden box waiting on her dresser.

It wasn't fancy. It didn't need to be. It held the only pieces that had ever mattered: two delicate heirlooms from her grandmother... and the ring Mac had given her.

She opened the box, breath catching in her chest, and set the bands inside. Keepsakes. Memories. Pieces of her. Pieces of them.

"We promised," she whispered, resting her fingers on the lid. "If anything happened, we'd move on. I swear, Mac—I'd have haunted your ass by now if you were still stuck on the sidelines."

She lifted her gaze—not to the ceiling, but to the space she held for him, the place where his absence had lived.

"I keep my promises. All of them. So stay your specter ass on whatever heavenly barstool they parked you at... and let me breathe again."

The lid clicked shut. Quiet. Final. But not painful—not anymore.

Steam followed her from the bathroom as she stepped out, wrapped in a lavender-scented towel. The mirror was fogged. For once, Sloane reached up and cleared it with the flat of her palm.

Not to critique or pick herself apart. But to see the woman looking back.

Her face wasn't as tight around the edges. She looked... different. No longer raw or fractured.

"You've got this," Sloane told her reflection, and the woman staring back seemed to agree.

She padded down the hallway barefoot, floorboards groaning in the spots she hadn't bothered to fix. The house wasn't perfect—hell, parts of it were worn and lopsided—but it was hers. Every nail, every scar, every quiet space she'd rebuilt alone. Two blocks from downtown and just close enough to catch the jukebox's echo if the windows were open.

She pulled on an old tee, the cotton clinging to her damp skin. The fabric felt soft and lived-in, like a hand on her shoulder guiding her to rest.

When she slipped under the covers, the sheets were cool, but her chest felt warm in a way it hadn't in a very, very long time.

Tonight was different. Tonight she'd said the truth out loud—really said it. And Daniel hadn't flinched or pitied her. He hadn't tried to fix her or talk her out of the moment.

He'd just... stayed.

That was enough for her to close her eyes without bracing for the darkness.

Chapter 2

♥

The bell over the door jingled, and Sloane didn't bother looking up—at first. But Sam's eyebrows went up, and that was all the warning she needed.

Daniel Rourke walked in, cutting across the empty stools like he'd been doing it for years.

Sam leaned in, voice low. "Well, that's new."

Sloane smirked into her glass. "Yeah. Mr. Clockwork just missed his cue."

Daniel skipped his usual seat—two stools down, the respectful distance he kept every week.

Today he sat beside her. He set the notebook down and flipped it open out of habit, pen in hand, the page staying blank.

"Afternoon," he said, his tone casual, his gaze a contradiction that she felt in her veins, like he knew exactly which rule he'd just broken.

Sloane cocked her head. "It's Wednesday."

"I noticed."

"Schedule slip?"

He folded his notebook shut and set it on the bar. "Adjustment."

Sam grinned wide enough to get smacked and retreated to the taps.

Sloane let the silence stretch, her smile sharp. "And what earned me an adjustment?"

Daniel's expression softened—not quite a grin, just enough to feel it. "You did. Last night."

She blinked once, hard. Oh.

He gave her no space to regroup. "Afraid I'd no-show next Tuesday," she asked, "or did you suddenly develop a craving for killer bar food as... luner?" She paused. "Lunch and dinner. You know. Luner. Never mind."

His brow lifted a fraction—his version of amused surprise. Her slip hung between them like bait.

"Afraid?" His voice stayed low, even. "I don't rattle easily."

He leaned an elbow on the bar, angling his body toward her—not crowding, just... claiming space.

"You shifted the ground yesterday," he said. "So I adjusted mine. Didn't seem smart to wait a week."

Sloane snorted—half laugh, half challenge. "So this is what? Dominance play? Desire? Or did you just crave Sam's overcooked fries for luner?"

Daniel's mouth curved again, sharper this time. "Maybe all three."

Sam barked a laugh from the taps. Sloane shot him a glare, but the twitch of her lips betrayed her.

Daniel held her gaze. "You make a move like you did last night—you don't pretend it evaporates. I'm here to see if you meant it."

Sam walked over and set a white takeout bag in front of her. Sloane grabbed it, stood, and tossed a twenty on the counter.

"Luner," she said again, holding his gaze like she was testing the weight of it. "I've got sketches to prep for tonight's client. Grab lunch and stop by; folks are friendly enough. But drop the cop energy—you'd be bad for business."

She tapped the bar twice. "Thanks, Sam. Tell Jonathan I've got that sketch for him."

Daniel stayed seated. He just sat there with one hand on his closed notebook. She felt his eyes following her as she lifted the bag, both shield and invitation.

"Luner," she said again, lips quirking as if daring him to correct her.

Daniel's mouth curved—slow, deliberate. "Not a cop," he said. "And if I stop by, I'll play by the house rules."

Her brows arched, skeptical but amused, and her boots were already carrying her toward the door, the white bag swinging at her side.

***

The sun hit her harder than she expected when she pushed out the door, the white bag warm in her hand. Her pulse thudded in her throat, her ears, everywhere but her wrist, where she tried to count it like she used to on scene.

Fuck. Fuck, fuck...

She could patch a gunshot, reset a shoulder, talk a car crash survivor back from the edge. But inviting him—Daniel—down to the shop? That was reckless. Amateur. Like passing a note in algebra at seventeen.

The shop door gave under her boot, the bell jangling overhead.

"Fuck."

Big Z glanced up from the half-finished sleeve in his chair, one brow rising. "New yoga mantra, Sloane?"

She managed a nod, throat too tight for anything else, and headed straight for her station. No more words—just her sketch pad, the hum of machines, and the riot in her chest she hoped no one else could hear.

Daniel turned on his heel before the shop door had even fully closed behind her. He stood on the sidewalk for a beat, then looked up at the "Baked Magic" sign.

He'd passed the bakery a hundred times and never gone in. Today he needed the excuse.

The smell hit him first—sugar, butter, warmth—nothing like the herbal-salt of Rosemary's, where fries and old stories lived in the wood. It gave him breathing room. Space to fold the jolt she'd given him at the bar into something that looked like logic.

He picked out two cannoli, three cookies, boxed and bagged in what appeared to be a signature midnight blue and silver box. The woman behind the glass case gave him a knowing smile, the kind that suggested she'd seen countless stories pass through her shop and filed them all away.

Dinner includes dessert, he told himself as he stepped back outside. A neat excuse. And if he showed up with cookies for her late-night sugar crash? That was casual enough.

Almost.

Except it wasn't casual. He knew her rhythm too well—that was the tell.

At first it had been caution. A woman alone, late, walking home. A professional instinct.

Now it was something else.

The bag warmed his hand as he crossed back to Flock of Ink. The street had thinned to its late-afternoon hush—delivery vans growling past, the hiss of half-dried pavement under tires. Her light was on. The soft amber glow haloed the sketches lining the walls inside.

He stepped in and let the door close slowly behind him.

Ink. Antiseptic. And something faintly floral she carried on her skin—something that didn't belong here and still worked.

Sloane didn't look up right away. She was bent over her sketch pad, pencil sweeping across the page like she was keeping tempo with a rhythm only she could hear.

Then, without turning: "You found dessert."

Daniel froze for half a second. The bag rustled when he set it on the counter. "I wasn't sure what you liked."

"Sugar," she said, finally glancing his way. "And quiet."

Her gaze flicked to the extra chair she'd pulled up beside her station—close enough for conversation, not quite close enough for contact. The invitation was subtle but intentional.

Something in his chest shifted.

He took the seat. The tattoo guns had gone silent; only the air filled the space between them.

"Didn't think you'd actually stop by," she said, flipping her pencil between her fingers.

"I wasn't sure I would," he admitted. "But you left an opening."

Sloane's mouth tilted—almost, almost a smile. "Careful, Rourke. I charge extra for therapy sessions."

He nodded toward the sketch pad. "Good thing I came for the art."

"Mm." Her eyes dipped to his forearm, then back up, deliberate. "Ever thought about ink?"

Daniel leaned back, meeting her gaze head-on. "I've spent a life avoiding permanence."

"Funny," she murmured, pencil tapping the page. "Most people come here looking for exactly that."

Her phone buzzed. A quick reschedule. A family emergency. Her big piece was pushed a few weeks out. A sudden hole in her night—rare.

She muttered a curse, then returned to her sketching. He stayed quiet this time. Just watched her hand move—steady, sure, controlled.

Then the bell jingled again. A walk-in. A woman with a well loved photo clutched in shaky hands.

Sloane's shift was instant. She greeted her gently, voice softening, posture easing. Daniel stayed in the background, blending into the hum of machines and ink.

He watched as the woman explained, voice cracking around the edges, and Sloane listened—really listened. Then she sketched. Fast. Intuitive. Sure.

When she slid the sketch across—a small bird carrying a pink ribbon in its beak—the woman's eyes filled.

"That's... her. That's Mom."

Sloane didn't smile. She just nodded once. "We can make it yours tonight if you're ready."

Daniel leaned back, silent.

He'd seen men defuse bombs and women stitch broken bodies back together. But he'd never seen someone carve grief into beauty with nothing but a pencil and quiet presence.

***

Daniel's car was idling at the curb outside Flock of Ink when she stepped out, helmet hooked on two fingers, jacket slung over her shoulder. "Thanks for the ride," she said, sliding into the passenger seat. "I really don't love walking home this late alone, even if it's only two blocks."

He didn't comment—just reached across her and clicked the seatbelt into place with a quiet snap. The closeness was brief, but his scent stayed: cedar, warm skin, and the faint masculine bite of good leather. Her pulse ticked once, sharp as a spark.

"And Z offered to change the oil first thing in the morning," she added, settling back. "He said his morning freed up. Hard to pass that up."

Daniel put the car into drive, giving her a sidelong look. "Good call."

The interior surprised her—clean, spacious, not a stray coffee cup or junk receipt in sight. The legroom alone was ridiculous. She stretched her boots out and still didn't hit the glove box. "Your car's huge inside," she muttered, surprised by her own honesty.

Daniel's mouth curved. "I travel a good bit. Space is handy."

"Mobile office of sorts," she nodded. "Makes sense."

The ride was quiet except for the low growl of the engine and the hum of fall wind sliding across the windows. It smelled like man, leather, and something warm she hadn't let herself want for a long time.

By the time he pulled up outside her house, the street had gone still—long shadows, cooling pavement, the soft rustle of leaves skittering across the gutter. Sloane hopped out, her boots thudding against the walkway. The porch light flickered the moment she stepped onto the top step—a weak pulse, a dying heartbeat.

She huffed. "Damn light again."

Daniel stopped beside her, gaze lifting. "How long's it been doing that?"

She shrugged, digging through her keys. "Few days. Week maybe. Thought it was Bruno."

His brow ticked. "Bruno."

"The ghost," she said dryly. "He flickers shit when he's bored."

Daniel watched her like he was sorting ghosts into categories—supernatural and the other kind. "You think I don't believe in ghosts?"

She lifted a shoulder. "Most people don't."

He stepped closer, heat brushing against her bare arm in the cool night air. "Oh, sweetheart..." His voice dropped, low and certain. "I've got a barn full. I just don't pretend they're all the supernatural kind."

Her breath caught—ghosts and spirits, two different things. He understood more than he was saying.

She swallowed, suddenly aware of how close he was.

Daniel reached out, slow but sure, and slid a finger beneath her chin, tilting her face up to his. Her breath caught—not because she was startled, but because something inside her had been waiting for this exact touch.

"Sloane," he murmured, voice rougher now, "you of all people know better."

His gaze flicked once to the flickering bulb, then back to her mouth. And then he kissed her.

Warm, steady, and unhurried—but charged beneath the surface, a low-voltage pull that stole the breath right out of her lungs. His mouth brushed hers once, then again, deeper the second time—like he was tasting permission, confirming the spark wasn't imagined at all.

Her lips parted on instinct. His hand slid to her jaw, thumb sweeping her cheek as he gathered her in, just enough to feel the heat jump between them.

She leaned in before she could stop herself—a small, involuntary press of want.

He answered it.

His lips pressed just a little firmer, his breath mingling with hers, a barely-there sound escaping him—low, almost a groan he swallowed before it could escape.

When he finally eased back, he didn't go far. He stayed close enough for her to feel the warm exhale against her mouth, close enough that her pulse couldn't decide whether to jump or melt.

Her eyes opened slowly, pupils blown wide. "Okay…" she whispered, the word slipping out without her permission.

She felt Daniel watch her like he could read every flicker behind her eyes, his thumb brushing her bottom lip once more, slower this time. "Yeah," he said quietly. "Okay."

Daniel's mouth curved, softer this time. A real smile. "Let's get you inside," he murmured, voice grazing her skin. "Before your neighbors start checking their porches."

She turned, pushing the door open. Warm light spilled across the entryway. "Timers," she admitted. "I… don't like coming home to a dark house. The music kicks on sometimes too. Makes the place feel lived in."

Daniel's expression softened in a way she'd never seen from him. "Smart," he said.

She stepped halfway into the doorway, hand braced against the frame. "You heading home?"

"Yeah." His voice dipped—steady, real. "But, Sloane?"

She froze.

"I want to see more of you."

She nodded, biting her lip without thinking. "I'd like that."

The corner of his mouth twitched—wolfish flicker—before he stepped back down the stairs. She closed the door softly, leaning against it for a moment until her breath evened.

***

Daniel didn't start the engine until he saw the hall light flip on. A warm square of yellow cut across the dark of her house—steady and sure.

Only then did he let out the breath he'd been holding. He hadn't realized he'd been waiting for that.

He schooled his expression, thumb brushing the steering wheel before he finally turned the key. The engine rumbled—low, controlled—like the pulse pounding behind his ribs.

Too close, he thought. Too damn close.

He hadn't meant to kiss her like that. Hadn't meant to let his restraint crack in the expanse of a heartbeat. But the second she looked up at him under that flickering porch light—wanting, wary, alive—reason didn't stand a chance.

She knew better. She wasn't naive or careless. So when she let him step into her orbit like that...he felt the trust in it like a live wire.

He gripped the wheel, knuckles whitening under the streetlights.

She'd said "okay" like it opened something—like letting him drive her home meant letting him past more than just her front door. That part he hadn't expected.

Her lip caught between her teeth. The tremor she tried to hide. The way her breath hitched when he lifted her chin. The flicker of the dying porch light. The way she whispered, *"I'd like that,"* like she wasn't sure she deserved wanting anything at all.

All of it replayed through him—not as images, but as a pull. Slow. Deep. Unavoidable.

He took the main road at a crawl, headlights sweeping long shadows across the asphalt. Deer season. Bad time to lose focus.

Especially with a woman like Sloane Calder still warm on his breath.

He flicked the vent toward him, the cool air brushing his chest, but it didn't touch the heat rolling under his skin.

He didn't even think about texting at a stoplight. Instead, he eased into the small lot by the corner store—the one that stayed open late for hunters and night-shift workers—and threw the car in park.

Reaching for his phone, thumb already tapping her name before he could overthink it.

Recommended porch lights with cameras—top three. Pick one. Tonight's bothered me.

He stared at the message, jaw tight. It wasn't enough.

He hesitated, then added:

Please.

He hit send before he could talk himself out of it.

Daniel didn't say please often. He tossed the phone onto the passenger seat and moved onto the road.

She had the windows lit when he left. Timers, she'd said. Music. A house that felt lived in.

Smart. Necessary.

But it wasn't enough. Not after seeing how dark that porch was. How tired she looked. How easily she brushed off danger, like she'd forgotten she wasn't made of iron.

The barn of ghosts he'd mentioned? They stirred now, restless.

He wanted to turn back. Knock on her door. Check her locks. Sweep her yard. Sit on her porch until sunrise just to make damn sure nothing touched her.

He didn't. He forced himself to drive home.

***

Sloane closed the door behind her and let her forehead rest against it, breath spilling out in a quiet, uneven rush. Gods.

She was really doing this...living again.

She moved on autopilot, pouring a glass of wine before carrying it to the bathroom. Steam curled up as she slipped into the tub, heat sinking into muscles she hadn't realized she'd kept clenched all day.

But her mind didn't settle.

Daniel. Quiet. Watchful. Reading everything without making a damn show of it.

The way he clocked the world. The way he clocked *her*.

That thought sent an unexpected spark skittering through her blood.

Her phone buzzed on the counter. A text.

Of course it was him.

Three porch-light replacements. Detailed. Practical. His recommendation highlighted at the top, two backups beneath it.

She smiled despite herself.

Too tired to overthink it, she tapped the first one. Then noticed express shipping kicked in if she ordered two.

Maybe it was the wine. Maybe the exhaustion. Maybe the way his kiss still lingered warm on her mouth—

—but something reckless slid up her spine.

> Ordered two, Sir. Front and back are covered.

The message sent with a soft chime.

Sloane dropped her head back against the tub edge and groaned into the rising steam. "Gods... what was I thinking?"

Later, shaking her head at the banter that followed, she dried off, pulled on a worn sleep shirt, and slid into bed without turning on the TV.

Her phone landed on the nightstand instead of her hand.

Halfway through fluffing her pillow, she paused.

She'd been present today—in a way she hadn't realized she'd stopped being.

A small smile tugged at her mouth. Annoying.

She turned off the lamp and tucked herself in, the house quiet, her thoughts steadier than usual.

***

Daniel was halfway up his driveway when his phone buzzed. He killed the engine but didn't move. Didn't breathe.

One thumb swipe—and her message lit the car.

Sir.

The word hit him low and hard, sharp enough to stop his breath—a clean shot straight to the place he didn't let anyone reach.

His grip tightened on the steering wheel until the leather creaked. A slow exhale dragged out of him, rough and unwilling.

Jesus.

Heat pulsed along his jaw.

He needed a minute before answering—because if he didn't take one, he'd say something he couldn't take back.

He scrubbed a hand over his mouth, trying to steady himself as the thought of her replayed in flashes: the way she'd looked after he kissed her the quiet want behind that single word

Fuck.

This wasn't the calm part of him. Not the professional part. Not the Tuesday-night regular.

This was the part he kept leashed—the part that noticed porch lights, checked locks, watched shadows, and wanted to stay close enough to feel her breathing.

Typed once. Deleted it. Typed again.

Finally, he let his thumb settle.

> Quick. Impressive. Good girl. I enjoyed watching you work tonight.

He stared at the screen, thumb hovering. He didn't push further. Just held the line she'd opened.

A moment later—

> Don't get used to it.

> Still impressed.

He could almost feel her stomach dip across the silence.

> Figured you would be. You drove me home like it was a mission.

> Behave, Sloane.

> ….

> Why start now?

His hand flexed on the wheel. He typed slower this time.

> Go to bed. Before you say something I can't ignore.

A pause. Measured. Charged.

Goodnight, Rourke.

Night, Sloane. Sleep with your doors locked.

He dropped his head back against the seat, a low feral sound slipping out—something not quite a laugh.

He was in trouble. The good kind. The dangerous kind. The kind he didn't walk away from.

Chapter 3

S loane realized anticipation had started heating her blood the moment her phone chimed.

She surprised herself by adding his contact—then again by assigning it a unique tone. Just for him.

He didn't send many words. Didn't need to. Every message came through clipped, controlled—steady.

She hated that she checked her phone more than usual.

> I'll be out of town for a few days. Work. You'll hear from me when I can.

No emojis. No fluff. Just information—threaded with something that felt like consideration.

> Copy that, Sir. Try not to yell at anyone.

He bit back a smile in a room where smiling didn't belong.

> Behave.

> Unlikely.

A beat.

> Lights arrived. Installing tomorrow. You can sleep now.

> Good timing. I'll be back by lunch.

> I've got tools. Don't need a handyman.

> Noted. Still would like to see you.

Her texts were always short—one-liners, sarcasm, the occasional photo of a half-finished sketch or a skull-covered coffee mug.

None of it should've mattered. Except it did.

He laughed every damn time. Laughed in briefings where laughter didn't live. Laughed so quietly he had to bite it down like a problem.

And then there was that *Sir* again—she managed to heat his blood from a thousand miles away.

And that's when he knew—

Sloane Calder was trouble in every way a man like him should avoid...and absolutely never would.

***

The new porch light sat half-installed, wires tamed neatly under her hands. Sloane balanced on the fifth rung of the ladder, denim stretching across her thighs, one boot braced on a step that had no business holding weight.

Daniel stood below, one hand steadying the ladder, the other resting on his hip.

"You know," he said, glancing up, "that angle's dangerous."

She didn't look down. "Which one? The ladder or your view?"

A deep, low sound rumbled in his chest—half warning, half amusement. "Careful, Sloane."

She smirked at the porch trim. "Why? Afraid I'll wake the beast?"

He answered without words. One hand steadied the ladder. The other delivered a slow, unapologetic swat across the curve of her ass.

Measured. Deliberate. A claim disguised as balance.

She nearly dropped the screwdriver.

"Hey—!" Her voice came out higher than she meant.

"You're leaning," he said, unbothered. "Kept you from falling."

"You kept me from—wow, okay." She blinked down at him. "You're unbelievable."

"Mm." He stepped back a few inches, arms folding across his chest. Then he reached for the ladder, watching her finish the job with quick, efficient movements.

Daniel took the screwdriver from her hand before she even realized he'd moved. He flipped the switch.

The light flared bright and steady.

The porch light glowed steady now, throwing warm light across the boards.

Daniel stepped back, hands on his hips, assessing it like he might any other job. "That'll do," he said.

"Told you," Sloane replied, brushing her palms on her jeans. Her pulse was still loud under her skin.

He glanced toward the street, then back at her." You busy?"

She arched a brow. "Depends. Why?"

"Trivia night at Rosemary's."

That got her attention. "You're branching out."

"Something like that." He glanced down the street, then back at her. "I figured if I was going to keep pushing my luck with you, I should probably stop pretending I'm in a hurry to be anywhere else."

She considered him for half a second—long enough to let that land. "Walk? Just two blocks," she said.

"The weather is perfect for it," he replied.

"Give me one second," Sloane said, already turning toward the door. "I need to turn the crock pot down to warm."

Daniel stayed on the porch, hands in his pockets, watching the glow from inside spill out through the window

***

The air had cooled just enough to be comfortable, the kind of evening that made walking feel intentional instead of like a chore.

Sloane locked the door behind them and started down the steps without looking back, confident he'd follow.

He did.

For a block, neither of them spoke. Footsteps. Distant traffic. Porch lights flicking on one by one.

"You do this often?" she asked eventually. "Trivia."

Daniel shook his head. "No."

She glanced at him. "You said that already."

"I meant it," he said. "I don't usually indulge in... fun."

That made her laugh. "You make it sound reckless."

"Sometimes it is."

She studied him as they walked. He wasn't watching the street so much as tracking everything—movement, light, people. Awareness without tension.

"What do you do when you're not working?" she asked. Casual. Not loaded.

He didn't answer right away. Not because he was avoiding it—because he was considering it.

"Depends on the day," he said finally. "Fix things. Read. Cook when I have time."

That surprised her. "You cook?"

"Better than I talk," he said.

She smiled. "That's yet to be tested."

They reached the corner and paused for a car to pass. He rested a hand at the small of her back—warm, gentle, protective.

"You?" he asked. "What do you do when you're not climbing ladders and antagonizing men on porches?"

"I like quiet," she said. "Music. Projects I don't finish. Good food."

"What kind of music?" he said.

Her brows lifted. "Good."

"Smartass," he replied easily.

That landed warmer than she expected.

Rosemary's came into view, windows glowing, familiar voices spilling onto the sidewalk. Normal. Lived-in.

"Last chance to bail," she said.

He held the door open for her, expression unreadable but steady. "I'm not going anywhere."

Sam looked up from behind the bar and grinned. "Well, hell. Look who brought company."

Sloane smiled back. "Don't get used to it."

Daniel nodded once, polite, already scanning for an open high-top.

Jonathan lifted his beer in greeting from the end of the bar. "Trivia team?"

"Apparently," Sloane said. "We're winging it."

***

Rosemary's was louder than it looked from the sidewalk—voices overlapping, chairs scraping, the low hum of anticipation that made the place feel awake instead of crowded.

Sam slid two menus onto the high-top and grinned. "Trivia starts in three. Scan the code, answer on your phone. Only touch it when the question's live."

Sloane scanned once, tapped her answer, then set her phone face-down on the table. Daniel mirrored the motion without comment.

Sam clocked it, pleased. "Drinks?"

"Whiskey," Sloane said. "Whatever's decent."

Daniel nodded. "Same. And fries. Wings."

"Sharing?" Sam asked, pen already moving.

Daniel glanced at Sloane. "Unless you object."

She smiled. "I never object to fries."

Jonathan appeared with a tired smile and a beer he clearly hadn't earned yet. "Team name?"

Sloane tipped her head toward Daniel. "You got anything?"

He leaned in, forearm brushing hers. "Let's see how the night goes."

"Bold," she said.

"Works," Jonathan muttered, already typing. "Team Bold."

She blinked. "Wait—"

Too late. He grinned and moved on.

A corner of Daniel's mouth lifted, "Bold, huh."

She shook her head, smiling. "Apparently anything I say is binding."

The first round rolled—general knowledge, a couple of easy wins. A music cue flashed that made Sloane snort softly into her glass.

"I know this one," she said. "My sister Kara played it on repeat when we were teenagers."

"Ah," Daniel said, mouth curving. "Relentless replays usually come with a sibling tax."

That did it.

Sloane laughed—deep and unguarded, the kind that tipped her forward until she had to brace a hand on the table, belly tightening as it shook out of her. It surprised her as much as it did him.

Sam set a basket down between them. "Fries and wings for Team Bold."

The moment shifted easily, the way good interruptions do.

Daniel watched her a beat longer than necessary, something easing in his expression.

Sam returned with the drinks and paused, eyes flicking between them. "Huh."

Sloane lifted a brow. "That obvious?"

"Trivia usually takes longer to warm people up," Sam said.

Jonathan snorted. "Some people are efficient."

Daniel lifted his glass. "Cheers to efficiency."

They clinked. Sloane's smile lingered as she reached for a fry.

Between questions, conversation filled the gaps without effort.

"You grew up here," Daniel said, casual, reaching for a napkin.

She nodded. "Born and raised. Sam and I went to school together. Both of us had a crush on Jonathan when he moved to town."

Jonathan groaned. "I was seventeen."

"And gorgeous," she said sweetly. "Still are."

Sam beamed like he'd won something.

Daniel laughed under his breath. "Fair."

"And you?" she said. "You don't feel new."

He shrugged. "My uncle lived here. I visited when leave allowed. Swung through every year or so."

"That's why," she said, recognition clicking. "Rourke. I knew the name sounded familiar."

"Yeah. He moved to be with my cousin. None of his kids wanted the house." Another shrug. "He offered. I bought it."

No drama. Just fact.

The pop-culture round flashed.

What 1987 fantasy comedy features the character Vizzini, famous for shouting 'Inconceivable!'?

Daniel answered instantly.

She turned toward him. "You didn't even hesitate."

"You know it."

"I absolutely do not."

His mouth curved. "We'll fix that."

He leaned in slightly. "Side bet. Next one I get right, you go on a formal date with me."

She laughed. "Confident."

"I'm observant."

"Fine," she said. "You win, I go."

The answer popped up.

Daniel was right.

She shook her head, smiling despite herself. "Well played."

"And if I get the next one," she added, already watching the screen, "I pick where."

"Deal."

The next question popped. He missed it.

"My place," she said without hesitation.

He accepted it easily, then added, "Next one, I pick the activity."

She lifted her glass. "You're on."

The screen refreshed.

Dirty Dancing.

She knew it. Knew it cold.

She didn't answer.

Daniel glanced at her—not surprised. Just aware.

His smirk was brief, satisfied. "Dinner and a movie."

She scoffed. "Of course."

"The Princess Bride," he added.

"But," she said, already reaching for another fry, "you're bringing the wine and dessert."

He laughed—low, real. "Done."

Jonathan slid their next drinks onto the table and leaned in. "Just so you know—you two are very obvious."

Sloane met Daniel's gaze, heat sparking again.

"Good," she said.

***

They stepped out of Rosemary's into air that had cooled more than she expected. The noise fell away behind them, replaced by the quieter rhythm of the street—distant tires, a laugh drifting from somewhere down the block.

Sloane shivered once, quick and reflexive, then laughed at herself.

"Oh, hell no," she said, already veering toward Baked Magic.

Daniel caught up in two strides. "Where are you going?"

She shot him a look over her shoulder. "What? It's cold. And Isadora makes the best hot chocolate ever."

He shook his head, amused, and followed her inside.

Warmth wrapped around them immediately—sugar and cocoa and something toasted. Isadora looked up from behind the counter, eyes brightening.

"Well, if it isn't trouble," she said, then glanced at Daniel. "Back so soon? I'll take that as confirmation the cannoli and cookies were a good pick."

Sloane grinned. "Daniel definitely scored points, courtesy of your magic."

Daniel laughed—easy, genuine. "Indeed. And I'll take two hot chocolates to go."

Isadora smiled knowingly as she turned back to the machine. "Coming right up."

Sloane rubbed her arms, more aware now of the chill she'd brushed off a minute ago.

Daniel noticed.

He didn't comment. He just slipped his jacket off and settled it over her shoulders, the weight of it steady and sure.

She stilled for half a second, then relaxed into it without thinking.

"Thank you," she said, quieter now.

He nodded once, like it was nothing at all.

They took their cups and stepped back out into the night, steam curling between them. A few steps down the sidewalk, her fingers brushed his.

Neither of them pulled away.

By the time she noticed, their hands were already linked—natural, unremarkable, exactly right.

She glanced up at him. He was watching the street ahead, thumb resting easy against her knuckles.

Something in her chest settled.

They walked the rest of the way like that, the night closing in around them, warmth shared, the quiet humming with everything they weren't rushing.

***

They reached her place without talking about it, hands still linked, steps slowing as the porch light came into view.

Sloane fumbled once with her keys, laughing softly at herself. Daniel steadied her wrist, warm and sure, then let go as the door swung open.

Inside, she tossed her keys into the bowl and set her empty cup beside it.

Daniel followed her lead, setting his cup inside hers.

The house held the quiet heat of earlier—warmth, spice, something slow and familiar beneath it all.

"Chili," he murmured, catching the scent as he stepped in behind her.

She smiled over her shoulder. "Yeah."

He nodded, listening to the quiet of the house. "Smells like fall—like something meant to warm you."

The door closed behind them with a muted click, and the world narrowed.

Daniel's hands came to her waist—no hesitation, no rush—guiding her back until her shoulders met the wall. The jacket slid open as he leaned in, mouth finding hers, deep and unrelenting, tasting whiskey and chocolate and her.

She made a sound low in her throat, fingers curling into his shirt, pulling him closer. His body pressed in, solid and undeniable, every intention right there between them.

Remember restraint, Rourke.

He kissed her again anyway—slower this time, deliberate—then eased back just enough to rest his forehead against hers, breath uneven.

"Tomorrow night," he said, voice rough with promise.

A beat.

"And if you don't feel like cooking," he added, softer now, "we'll order in."

His mouth brushed hers once more, a final, lingering kiss meant to stay.

"But that chili?" A faint smile. "Perfect for tomorrow."

He stepped back before either of them could say something they weren't ready to keep.

Sloane watched him go, still wrapped in his jacket, pulse loud in her ears.

She locked the door behind him, releasing a breath she hadn't realized she'd been holding.

Her hand came to her chest, fingers pressing lightly as if to steady something still moving there.

Daniel stayed there a moment longer after the door closed, the taste of their kiss still sharp on his tongue.

Tomorrow.

He rolled his shoulders once, steadying himself, then headed down the steps with a purpose that hadn't been there before.

Inside the car, he sat for a beat before starting it, hands resting on the wheel. The street was empty—just the hum of the engine and the soft glow of porch lights down the block.

"Note to self," he said as the car rolled forward, voice low and even. "Call Isadora in the morning. Hot chocolate tonight means she'll want something warm tomorrow. Ask what her favorite is."

A pause.

"And pick up the bourbon-barrel cab. The good one."

He exhaled, a small smile pulling at his mouth.

"Tomorrow night," he added, then pulled away from the curb, the road ahead clear.

Chapter 4

D aniel stood on her porch with the kind of patience that came
from wanting something—and choosing not to rush it.

When the door opened, Sloane's face lit instantly.

Her gaze dropped to the box in his hands—then back to him.

"Well," she said, eyes bright, voice low with delight, "I see you came
prepared."

He lifted it slightly, a corner of his mouth curving. "Dessert."

The box was unmistakable.

Deep night-sky blue. Not black—richer than that. Flecked with
silver stars, *Baked Magic* pressed cleanly across the lid like a promise.

Sloane made a soft sound in the back of her throat, already reaching
for it. "Oh, you understood the assignment."

She leaned in and kissed his cheek—quick, warm, approving—then
relieved him of the box like it was already hers.

Daniel chuckled, genuine amusement in it. Mission accomplished.

Inside, she led without looking back, already opening the lid on the
counter as if checking proof.

He followed her in, closing the door behind him, the house wrapping around them in warmth and scent.

Her house smelled like chili and cumin and toasted corn-meal—rich, grounding, the kind of warmth that settled into a man's bones.

But what stopped him wasn't the food.

It was the room itself.

A soft throw draped over the couch, worn thin at the edges from use. A stack of books on the coffee table—dog-eared, not decorative. A mug beside them, a faint lipstick print on the rim. Lamps instead of overhead lights, casting a low gold glow. Fuzzy socks half-kicked under the armchair. A plant in the corner she was clearly trying—and failing—to keep alive.

It was all so her.

And it landed harder than he expected.

She glanced over her shoulder, pleased. "Cornbread's almost done."

He set the wine bottle on the counter. "Where do you keep the corkscrew?"

"Second drawer," she said. "Left."

He found it easily, working the cork loose with practiced calm. The soft pop landed between them like punctuation.

She watched him pour, leaning back against the counter now, the box tucked protectively at her side.

"Bourbon-barrel cab," he said. "Thought it might hold its own."

Her smile deepened. "You did good, Rourke."

He handed her a glass. "I had all day to think about it."

"Tell me I don't need a tiara or glass slippers for tonight's movie," she said, sipping to taste.

Daniel stepped in behind her, slow and deliberate, close enough that the warmth of his chest brushed her shoulder blades.

"That tone," he murmured near her ear. "Careful what you invite."

He planted one palm on the counter beside her hip, angling his body toward hers.

She froze—just for a breath—then sipped her wine again.

He huffed a quiet laugh and moved into the living room while the timer ticked down.

When it beeped, she plated the cornbread and chili and carried everything over. Daniel was on his phone, thumbs moving with surgical precision.

"Hey," she said, setting his plate down. "No work at the table."

He didn't look up.

"Not work."

He held out his hand.

"Password?"

She gave it without thinking, already turning back for napkins. By the time she returned, he'd finished.

"Cameras are set," he said as she sat. "App's on your network. You'll just need to link your phone."

Her brows lifted. "You did all that in five minutes?"

"Yes."

His answer didn't waver.

"Should I be worried?"

"No."

He let the silence stretch just long enough—

"Unless you installed them wrong," he added, mouth curving.

She laughed, shaking her head. "Only if you distracted me too much, smartass."

He passed her the phone. "You want me to walk you through it, or do you trust me to finish?"

She buttered her cornbread. "You can do it. I have my skills. You have yours."

Something shifted in his gaze at that—subtle, but real.

"You do," he said quietly.

She cleared her throat. "So... you have access now?"

"For the moment," he said evenly. "Once setup's done, it locks to you. I only have admin access for initialization."

"Oh."

"If you want," he added, "I can route it through my service. Friends-and-family rate. Better encryption. Only if you ask. I won't monitor anything. It's your system."

He saw it in the way her shoulders eased, the tension slipping loose like she'd set something down she'd been carrying too long.

"Thank you," she said softly.

"It's security, Sloane," he replied. "Not surveillance."

Her pulse jumped.

She leaned back into the couch, smirk returning like she'd never lost it.

"So what, Rourke? I'm safe now?"

His gaze sharpened.

He took a slow sip of wine.

"Not yet," he said.

"But safer than you were."

Heat curled low in her belly.

She took a bite of chili, pretending not to feel it.

"Careful," she said lightly. "You keep talking like that, and I'll think you're trying to impress me."

His smile was slow. Wolfish.

"Maybe I am."

***

The chili was still hot enough to demand her attention, which was probably for the best.

Sloane slid her bowl aside and reached for her wineglass instead.

Daniel was already there, lifting the bottle, watching the level as he poured—unhurried, deliberate.

The scent bloomed between them, dark fruit and oak.

"Save room," he said, nodding toward the box from Baked Magic.

She smiled. "I always do."

"You cooked," he said. "I've got the dishes."

She snorted. "Yeah, okay."

He stood and reached for her bowl.

Sloane's brows rose—surprised—but she masked it with a smirk as she gathered the bread plates—

only for Daniel to take them straight out of her hand.

"Rourke—?"

"You cooked," he repeated evenly. "I've got this."

He stepped past her, letting his body skim hers in a slow, deliberate pass before he set dishes in the sink. He reached for the sponge with infuriating calm.

Sloane stared for a second—blink, blink—before her instinctive need to stay in motion kicked back in.

"Fine," she muttered, crossing to the stove. "I'll put up the leftover chili."

She lifted the pot with practiced ease, poured the contents into a container, sealed it with a click...and carried the pot back toward the sink.

Daniel glanced over his shoulder. "You don't have to—"

She slapped the empty pot onto the counter beside him, hands on her hips.

"Have at it," she said. "I have a thing for domestic men."

The grin that followed was sharp and wicked—the kind meant to test someone's temperature.

Daniel stilled.

"Sloane," he said slowly, eyes narrowing, "you're making some bold assumptions about my skill set."

She shrugged, leaning back against the counter like she hadn't just struck a match.

"I mean..."

Her fingers flicked toward the sponge in his hand.

"Then by all means," she said lightly. "If the apron fits."

His head lifted. Brows rose.

Oh. She liked that.

Her grin deepened. There it was—the playful spark she hadn't felt alive inside her in a long, long time.

Daniel set the sponge down slowly.

He turned toward her fully, leaning a hip against the counter, crossing his arms in a slow, unhurried display of male patience that was somehow hotter than any wall-pin or kiss he'd given her yet.

"Sloane," he said quietly, "you're trying very hard to get a reaction out of me."

She blinked once, lips curving. "Am I?"

"Yes." No hesitation.

She laughed. A real laugh—sharp and bright.

"And is it working?"

Daniel stepped closer—two slow, measured steps—until her back grazed the counter and his body made the space feel smaller. Close enough that she could feel the heat of him through his shirt and breathe in the quiet warmth of his skin. Clean. Masculine. Nothing but him.

His voice dropped an octave. "You know damn well it is."

Her breath caught.

"Careful," he murmured, eyes flicking down to her mouth and back up. "I'm patient. I'm controlled. But you keep poking like that... and you're going to find out exactly what kind of man you're teasing."

She swallowed—hard. Her fingers curled around the counter's edge.

"And what kind is that?" she whispered.

Daniel's eyes lit—a wicked promise.

"The kind who doesn't mind a challenge..." He leaned in, his breath brushing her cheek— "...but doesn't lose."

Her heart pounded so hard she felt it in her palms.

He pulled back just enough to let her breathe, letting the promise hang between them like heat off pavement.

Then—with infuriating control—he picked the sponge back up.

"Let me finish the dishes," he said, turning back to the sink. "Before you get yourself in trouble."

She exhaled shakily. "Trouble?" she echoed.

Daniel didn't look at her. "Mm-hm." He rinsed a bowl. "You're already halfway there."

***

The sink went quiet behind her.

Sloane wiped the counter, slid the chili into the fridge, then reached for the coffee she'd brewed out of habit. She hesitated—then opened the cabinet, smiling to herself as she found the Irish cream.

Two mugs. Equal pour. Deliberate.

The low clink of a dish set to dry. A final rinse. Footsteps sounded down the hall—unhurried, familiar now.

She carried the mugs into the living room and had just settled onto the sofa when Daniel appeared in the doorway, sleeves pushed up, hands still damp.

He paused when he saw the mugs.

"Peace offering?" he asked.

"Maybe," she said lightly, holding one out. "Is it working?"

He took it, inhaled. "Irish coffee."

"You order it almost every Tuesday," she said. "Figured if tonight's a date, I should act like I notice things."

Something in his expression shifted—quiet, deliberate. He took a sip, eyes never leaving her.

"You do."

He crossed the room then, easy and unhurried, and sat beside her—close enough that his thigh found hers without apology.

The opening credits of *The Princess Bride* glowed on the screen.

"Don't get smug," she said. "I lost a bet. This doesn't mean I'm emotionally prepared."

His arm stretched along the back of the couch. His knee stayed pressed to hers.

"You'll survive," he said. "Probably quote it later without realizing."

She snorted. "Unlikely."

"We'll see."

He settled deeper beside her, his forearm grazing her shoulder as he did.

The touch warmed her skin instantly, a slow heat that knocked her breath just slightly out of rhythm.

Sloane lifted her Irish coffee like it was armor.

"Comfortable?" she asked, aiming for bored.

His gaze moved over her—the rise of her breath, the warmth creeping up her throat, the way she angled toward him even as she pretended not to.

"I am," he said. "You've created a relaxing home." His voice dropped a shade lower.

She shifted her leg—an innocent adjustment—but the movement pulled her closer, her hip brushing his.

A shiver slid down her spine.

His attention sharpened. She could feel it—the quiet intensity of it—the way his focus seemed to lock in, like he was tracking something she hadn't meant to reveal.

His fingers touched her upper arm, tracing a slow line along her skin.

Her breath caught before she could stop it.

"You cold?" he asked softly.

"I'm fine," she lied, staring harder at the TV.

He leaned in—a breath closer, his presence slipping down her nerves like warm electricity.

"You keep saying that," he murmured.

She swallowed. "Movie's getting good."

Daniel didn't look at the screen.

His gaze dropped to her wrist resting on her thigh.

Her pulse jumped beneath her skin—visible, undeniable.

His hand moved—slow, deliberate—the warm drag of his knuckles along the inside of her wrist.

Heat shot through her like a live current.

"Tell me something," he murmured, his touch following the rhythm of her pulse. "When you're nervous... does your pulse always jump like that?"

Her breath stuttered.

"You're imagining things."

Daniel's fingers closed around her wrist—gentle but sure—holding her still, capturing the beat of her pulse in his palm.

The contact alone made her breath hitch.

"No," he said, voice low and certain. "I see you."

His thumb pressed lightly into the inside of her wrist, and her body responded before she could stop it—heat racing up her arm, into her chest, everywhere.

She nearly spilled her coffee.

"You know exactly what you're doing," she whispered, her voice shaking.

Daniel leaned in, lips brushing the edge of her ear—barely a touch, but enough to unravel her.

"I think you want me to," he breathed.

Her chest rose too fast.

Her thighs pressed together instinctively.

The way his attention deepened told her he noticed—every breath, every tell she couldn't hide.

***

He stayed close— close enough that her body angled toward him on instinct, close enough that every remaining boundary hummed like a live wire. His thumb lingered at her pulse, a steady warmth anchoring the moment. The movie kept playing, sound and color blurring into background noise. Sloane's focus narrowed to breath, heat, and the man beside her.

Sloane swallowed hard. "So you're gonna keep testing me?"

Daniel's fingers slid up her arm—slow, deliberate— a long stroke that felt like a command written on skin. "I test what I want to understand," he said. "And do you understand me?" she shot back.

Daniel's smile was the kind that melted resolve— dark, slow, devastating. "Not yet," he murmured, leaning in, hand sliding into her hair, fingers curling at the base of her skull. "But I'm getting close."

She turned toward him, heart hammering. "Daniel..."

His breath touched her mouth— one inch, one breath, one heartbeat away from hers. "Sloane," he murmured, voice rough, "Tell me to stop."

She didn't. Couldn't.

Daniel's thumb held her pulse at her wrist, his breath warming her cheek. Sloane's fingers curled in his shirt, pulling, needing, her resolve worn thin by heat, by the way his breath never left her skin. "Daniel..." she whispered—

His hand slid from her wrist to her jaw, tilting her face with a precision that didn't allow escape. His mouth brushed hers once— and when she inhaled sharply, lips parting, he closed the distance like a man starving.

He took her mouth, sealed her breath with his, and kissed her slow at first—testing, coaxing, learning— then deeper, hotter, memorizing her, mapping the shape of her want, making a vow with every stroke of his tongue.

Her hand slid up his chest, gripping his shoulder— anchoring him there— until she was half on his lap and everything else blurred away.

A low growl slipped from him when her breath caught. His hand fisted gently in her hair, guiding her, the other gripping her hip, pulling her against him until her breath broke.

She gasped— he swallowed it, deepening the kiss, owning every inch of her surrender.

She tried to speak— but he stole it with another kiss, slower this time, agonizing in its tenderness. Her hands trembled where they clutched him. Her body answered before her mind could.

Her hands slid to the back of his neck, holding him there. He broke the kiss only long enough to rest his forehead against hers, their breaths tangling in the heat.

"Sloane..." His voice raw. "Yeah?" she whispered, eyes blown wide.

"This—" His jaw tightened— "—is going to be a problem."

A breathless laugh escaped her. "Good. I like problems."

He crushed his mouth to hers again— rougher now, hungrier— She went rigid against him for half a second—then melted.

His hands slid lower. The room spun. She forgot how to breathe properly. His rhythm stuttered, like thought had just short-circuited.

Daniel's kiss devoured her, giving her no time to recover. He shifted, sliding his palm up her ribs— fingertips grazing skin that hadn't been touched in a year. She stilled, then moved into him without thinking.

"Look at me," he breathed against her mouth. She did. Gods help her, she did.

His eyes were blown wide— heat, hunger, and something deeper... recognition. Dragging his thumb across her lower lip. Her body arched involuntarily, heat spiking through her veins.

"Sloane..." Her name came out like a vow. A surrender. A claim.

She grabbed the front of his shirt, fisting the fabric, dragging him down with a mix of desperation and fury and want. "Daniel—"

He kissed her hard, committing her taste to memory in case he never got another chance.

One hand anchored at the back of her neck, the other slid beneath her thigh, lifting her effortlessly the rest of the way into his lap.

Her breath hitched as her hips settled against him. Her legs wrapped around his waist.

He groaned—low, guttural— mouth sliding from her jaw to her throat, her shoulder, his lips lingering where her pulse jumped.

His hands found the hem of her shirt, pushed it up without breaking the kiss, fabric catching briefly at her arms before it was gone, tossed aside and forgotten.

"You have no idea what you're doing to me." His voice shook against her skin.

She smiled, reckless and breathless. "Oh, I think I do."

He growled— an honest, visceral sound— and kissed her again, deep and consuming, until the world dropped away.

His fingertips tracing her spine, a cry slipped from her. "Sloane... fuck..."

He lifted his head just enough to see her— really see her— and something in his face shifted. Hunger still burning, but clamped down hard, like he'd just made a decision he couldn't unmake.

Her hand cupped his jaw, thumb brushing his cheek. "Daniel..."

He kissed her slow— intimate— His forehead touched hers. "I'd walk through fire for you," he breathed, like it slipped out, like he didn't mean to say it aloud but couldn't stop it.

"Don't say that," she whispered, voice breaking.

He held her face in both hands, thumbs tracing her cheekbones. "I already mean it."

She kissed him again, deep and trembling, as his hands roamed her hips, her ribs, the lines of her body— memorizing her like she might vanish.

He kissed her shoulder. Her throat. Her collarbone. Sloane trembled beneath him.

His hands framed her face, steadying her like she might bolt. "Sloane," he murmured against her lips, "tell me you feel this."

Her breath hitched—

BUZZ—

The sound tore through the room, sharp and wrong. It wasn't his regular phone. She felt the shift instantly—the way his body locked, the way his jaw set.

***

Daniel's entire body went rigid beneath her— the kind of tension she'd only seen in men waiting for bad news on a radio line. He stayed still at first. Just breathed once through his nose, a controlled inhale that told her everything had changed.

Sloane felt her chest hollow.

Reaching into his pants pocket without breaking eye contact, he pulled out a matte-black flip phone. He snapped it open. "Rourke." His voice dropped—gravel and steel.

A pause. Tight. Heavy. His jaw ticked once—the only crack in the armor. "Copy." Another breath. "No, not alone."

Sloane's pulse spiked. As silence stretched, her stomach twisted as she wrapped the throw that had fallen from its spot around her like armor.

He listened with his eyes half-closed, every muscle pulled tight as if memorizing details. "I'll be there in twenty." He snapped the phone shut. Sharp. Final.

Sloane swallowed hard. "What was—"

Daniel stood with that controlled precision she'd only ever heard soldiers described with— the man who'd just kissed her like she was oxygen replaced by someone colder, focused, a wall of trained intent.

"I have to go," he said. His voice flat. Neutral.

Her breath hitched. "Is it bad?"

His eyes flickered—a bare flash of conflict— before the shutters slammed down again. "Yeah." A beat. "But it's my job." Another beat. "And it's nothing for you to worry about."

He hated the lie—she could hear it in the way softness strangled his voice the instant it slipped out.

Sloane moved toward him, barely a shift, but enough. "Daniel."

He froze. "This is what you do?" she whispered. "No warning?"

He swallowed, throat tight. "I haven't had anyone to warn," he said quietly. "Not in a long time."

Her breath broke.

He stepped closer—just one step— and cupped the side of her neck with a hand that was warm and shaking in ways he would never admit aloud. "I'll be back." His thumb brushed her jaw once—quiet claim. "Understand?"

A beat. "I. Will. Be. Back."

She swallowed. "When?"

"When I'm done."

"Days?"

Daniel hesitated—the silence answering for him. It landed like a blow. Her throat tightened. "Daniel…"

He closed his eyes for a single heartbeat— then opened them with resolve men carry only when walking toward danger they expect to meet head-on.

He cupped the back of her neck, rested his forehead against hers, and breathed her in like it was the only breath he'd get tonight. "I'm coming back," he said, voice low and fierce.

Then he let her go. Because if he didn't—he never would.

Her breath stuttered. He stepped back. Turned. Opened the door.

Then paused— hand braced on the frame, shoulders broad, silhouette carved out by the porch light he'd told her to replace.

Without looking back: "You're the first thing I'll think about when this is over."

And then he was gone.

The door clicked shut— quiet, final.

Sloane stood in the silence he left behind, fingers pressed to her lips where his had been, the empty room pressing in, and the fear of losing something she'd only just allowed herself to want clawing up her throat.

***

Daniel hit the ignition too hard. The engine roared, headlights slicing through the dusk — but his pulse was louder.

He gripped the wheel, jaw locked, muscles trembling in a way he hadn't felt since the sandbox.

It wasn't fear or adrenaline.

It was her.

Sloane fucking Calder.

Her taste still on his tongue. Her breath in his lungs. Her pulse still hammering against his thumb.

He tried to breathe — slow, steady, how he'd trained himself to —but the memory of her lips brushing his throat shattered the rhythm every damn time.

"Fuck," he muttered, slamming the car into gear.

He shouldn't have kissed her like that. Shouldn't have touched her—shouldn't have let her climb into his lap like she belonged there.

But god — she did.

He could still feel the curve of her waist under his hands, the tremor in her breath, the way she whispered his name like she'd been holding it back for months.

And the look in her eyes—holy hell—that look cut straight through him, clean and merciless.

He pulled onto the main road too fast. Tires caught, jerked, steadied.

He didn't care.

The phone call replayed in his head:

Coordinates. Timeline. Ingress. Egress. Watch your six. No comms.

He'd done this a thousand times. In. Out. Don't look back.

But he had looked back tonight. He'd almost turned around. Almost told them to find someone else.

Because for the first time in his life —

He had someone to come back to.

His fingers flexed on the wheel, remembering the feel of her neck under his palm, the way she leaned into the kiss like she had a right to him —and a groan punched out of him.

He raked a hand through his hair "Jesus, Rourke. Pull your shit together."

But he couldn't. Not fully.

Because leaving her standing in that living room felt wrong in a way that had nothing to do with the mission.

She'd looked at him like he was stepping into fog and she wasn't sure he'd come back out.

And him?

He hadn't had the presence of mind to tell her what she needed to hear.

He should've told her he'd be off comms. Should've told her not to worry. Should've told her he'd contact her the second he could.

But her mouth had still been warm against his. Her breath had still been shaking. He'd been undone and thinking with parts of himself he didn't use around civilians.

So he walked out. He promised he'd be back. And then he left her blind.

The realization hit mid-turn, hard enough to make him grip the wheel like it might break.

"Goddamn it."

She'd worry. Of course she'd worry.

Her voice echoed in his head:

"Days?"

And he'd given her nothing.

He'd seen enough widows to recognize the shape of a woman bracing for a call that never comes. And Sloane was already cracked from losing Mac —he felt it in every tremor, every inhale, every shield she tried to hide behind.

He cursed again, long and low.

He wanted to text her—tell her to breathe, that he'd be fine, that—

But his personal phone was off. Protocol. Non-negotiable. No exceptions.

He hated that tonight. For the first time in his life, he hated protocol.

Daniel swallowed hard, eyes locked on the black highway unwinding before him.

He didn't make vows.

He noted the mistake.

When he came back, he'd do better—or he'd step away before he caused more damage.

He focused on the road. In. Out. No mistakes.

Chapter 5

The latch clicked shut and Sloane simply stood there, suspended in the hollow he'd left behind. For several heartbeats she didn't breathe, didn't think, didn't move—only listened as the echo of his boots faded down the porch steps, each one tugging something vital out of her chest that she hadn't realized she'd started to reclaim.

Only when the engine caught and roared did her lungs finally drag in air—shallow, uneven, like surfacing too fast from black water. She walked back into the living room on legs that felt heavier with every step, reached for the remote without looking, and silenced the TV. The quiet rushed in, too complete, too edged, turning the room into something haunted even though nothing had died in it yet.

In the kitchen she opened the cabinet on autopilot, bypassed the wine, and pulled down the whiskey. Poured it neat. "Fuck," she whispered to the counter, the word cracking open in her throat before the liquor even touched it.

She carried the glass to the sofa, body moving while her mind stayed frozen in the doorway where he'd promised to return. She didn't think; she simply sank into the exact corner where he'd held her, dragged the blanket over her shoulders, and pressed it to her face like it could substitute for breath. Gods, his scent was still there—warm skin, exhaled heat, the ghost of the kiss that had unraveled her so thoroughly she could still feel it lodged under her ribs. A raw sound slipped out of her, too broken for a sob, too jagged to pass for steady.

"I'll be back," he'd said. But no when. No unreachable. No mission parameters. Just a promise stripped of edges, no shape to grip in the dark.

She curled tighter, knees drawn up, blanket wrapped like armor she didn't trust. Her pulse wouldn't settle—it kept climbing, stuttering, bracing for a blow that had already landed. She tried logic in small, desperate doses: he'll text, he'll call when he can, he meant it, he has to. Her phone stayed face-down on the coffee table, screen black, offering nothing.

Every few minutes her gaze drifted to it anyway, waiting for light that refused to come. She pulled the blanket higher, tucked her chin inside, inhaled as deeply as she dared. His scent struck again—sharp, devastating, familiar in a way that made her want to laugh and shatter at once. She was in so much trouble.

Whiskey warmed her throat but couldn't reach the cold blooming through her chest. She didn't even try for the bedroom. The thought of leaving this room, this exact place where his arms had last closed around her, felt like betrayal. So she stayed—lights off, knees to chest, his scent pressed under her nose, heart lodged high in her throat—her whole body coiled around the terror of wanting a man who spoke danger like his native tongue.

Her eyes stung. She refused the tears anyway. Not for someone she'd barely had time to claim. But the ache didn't ask permission.

Fingers curled white-knuckled into wool. Breath trembled in shallow bursts. Into the dark she whispered, barely audible, "Don't leave me."

Sleep arrived in fragments, shallow and restless. She woke still curled the same way, blanket fisted in her hands, heart still braced for footsteps that never returned. At some point she stopped pretending she would move to the bed. Stopped pretending any of this was temporary. By the third night the blanket had staked its claim on the sofa. So had she.

***

It had been days. Nearly a week.

Sloane stared at her phone for what felt like the hundredth time that morning, the screen still stubbornly blank. No missed calls. No messages. Not even a goddamn delivery update.

She tried again. Voicemail. Straight to it. His recorded voice—flat, impersonal—scraped against her nerves like sandpaper. She swallowed hard, throat tight. "What the hell are you doing, Rourke...?"

Text instead. Porch light is on. I'm safe. —sent.

She waited. Ten minutes. An hour. Two. Nothing.

Later: Back light and camera installed. A+ for the rec. —sent.

Still nothing.

The next morning, after another night of staring at the ceiling until her eyes burned: Ready for your first ink. Thought of something we talked about. (as if they'd talked about anything except wanting each other) Delivered. Read? No way to know.

Silence.

Finally, a text that shook out of her before she could polish it, before she could pretend she wasn't terrified: R U OK? —delivered.

And then the crushing, suffocating nothing that followed.

Her chest tightened in that old, terrifying way—not fresh grief, not memory, but instinct. The kind that tells a woman something is terribly, irrevocably wrong.

She paced the living room, trying to shake the rising panic out of her limbs. "Stop it," she muttered, fists clenching, unclenching. "Stop. He told you he'd be back. Someone would call if—"

She cut herself off before the sentence could finish. Refused to chase that thought to its end.

She scrubbed the kitchen until the counters gleamed. Put on music, too loud. Turned it off. She opened the fridge. Closed it. Opened it again—then shut it harder.

She reorganized drawers she'd reorganized last week. Did laundry she didn't need. Cleaned her brushes. Scrubbed the bathroom tile until her arms trembled.

Nothing helped.

The next day she deep-cleaned the shop top to bottom, even though Kerry's wife had already done it yesterday. By the time Big Z walked in, she was halfway up a ladder dusting vents she'd never cared about before.

He eyed her like she was a bomb wired wrong. "You good?" he rumbled.

She didn't look down. "I'm fine."

His grunt said bullshit. His eyes said worried.

"Z…" Her voice cracked—the tiniest fracture. She swallowed it down. "You hear anything? About—anything?"

He didn't answer. His jaw tightened. A small shake of his head. Not here. Not now. Not with walls that listened.

Her stomach dropped. Hard.

By the sixth night she'd polished her bike twice. Her house smelled like disinfectant instead of her. She hadn't slept more than a restless hour at a time. Couldn't eat more than a few bites. Every breath scraped like something was lodged beneath her ribs.

Every time she closed her eyes, he was there—in a ditch or a doorway or bleeding out where no one could find him, phone smashed, radio dead, breath slowing, no help coming.

She pressed her nails into her palms to stop the images. "He said he'd be back," she whispered, pacing. "He said—"

The words cracked apart in her throat. The panic crawled higher, colder, sharper, refusing to be reasoned with.

So she did the only thing she knew that could quiet the noise for a few hours. She pulled on boots. Intending for a ride to clear her mind, instead she ended up at Rosemary's. Took a booth instead of her usual stool—somewhere tucked away, somewhere small, somewhere she didn't have to pretend she wasn't unraveling.

By the third whiskey, she wasn't even sure what she was trying to drown anymore— fear, hope, or the image of a man with gravel in his voice promising he'd come back and then disappearing anyway.

***

The second Daniel switched his personal phone back on, it blew up in his hand. Missed calls. Texts. Her name, over and over. Sloane. Sloane. Sloane.

Every message landed like a blow to the ribs. Porch light is on. Ready for your first ink. R U OK? Daniel? Where are you? Please.

His chest tightened so hard he braced a hand on the car door. "Fuck."

He hit her contact immediately. Voicemail. Again. Still voicemail. His throat went raw. "Pick up, Sloane. Come on, pick up."

Text: I'm back. I'm okay. Call me. Unread.

He tried again. Still unread. The silence crawled under his skin.

A slow, gut-deep panic settled—the kind he hadn't let himself feel since the night things went sideways overseas. He never panicked. Never.

He called Big Z. The older man answered on the second ring, voice a low growl. "About damn time."

Daniel flinched. "Where is she?"

"You tell me," Z snapped. "She called asking questions she shouldn't be asking. You left her blind, Rourke. She's been tearing herself apart for days."

Guilt shot through him, sharp and vicious. "I didn't—I had to kill my phone. Protocol. I didn't think—"

"No shit you didn't think." Z's voice dropped, dangerous and cold. "You fix it. Or you leave her the fuck alone."

Daniel swallowed hard. "I intend to."

"Good." A beat. "Because she deserves better than ghosts."

The line went dead.

Daniel sat in the driver's seat, breathing through the shame and the nauseating realization of how badly he'd fucked this up. She'd worried. Of course she had. He'd seen the shadows in her eyes before he left. He should have told her. Should have warned her. Too late.

He called Sam. The bartender answered soft—too soft—and Daniel's stomach flipped. "She's here."

Daniel squeezed the phone until his knuckles burned. "Is she okay?"

"No." A pause. "Booth in the back. Not her usual place. Third whiskey."

Daniel closed his eyes. Fuck.

Sam's voice dropped lower. "Don't destroy her. She doesn't deserve heartbreak again."

Daniel swallowed the instinct to argue. "Last thing I want. Last fucking thing."

"Then fix it," Sam said. "And Rourke?" "What." "Don't make her chase you."

Daniel hung up without responding.

He sat for one breath. Two. Three.

Then he exploded into motion. "Fuck this."

He shoved the car into gear and tore out of the lot, gravel spitting behind him as he shot toward Rosemary's with only one thought burning through his head:

Let her yell. Let her curse me. Let her hit me. Just let her be there.

He could take her fury. He could take her disappointment. He could take her walking away if that's what she needed.

But he couldn't take her being broken and alone because of him.

He would fix this—or walk out of her life forever if that's what kept her safe. But he would see her. Tonight. No matter what it tore open inside him.

***

The booth sat half-shadowed in the back corner, tucked far enough away that no one would notice unless they knew to look. Sloane wasn't a booth person—too boxed in, too static—but tonight the stool felt too exposed. Too ritualistic. Too much like waiting at an altar for someone who might never return.

So she slid into the corner, jacket bunched beside her like a barricade. Sam set her third whiskey down, eyebrows knitting with concern but his voice soft. "No lectures. Just hydrate so you don't feel like shit tomorrow."

A glass of water clinked onto the table, followed by a packet of electrolytes. "Serious, Sloane. Or I'll call Jonathan and let him go full resident intern on your ass."

She huffed something between a laugh and a groan. "You're a menace, you know that?" But her hand closed around the water anyway.

The bell over the door jingled. She didn't look up. Daniel did.

His gaze swept the room once—quick, efficient, trained—caught her bike still parked out front, then cut straight to her booth. A single look at her posture—too still, too quiet, too bright around the eyes—and something in him clicked over.

He crossed the room without hesitation, sliding into the opposite side of the booth like it had been waiting for him. "Not your usual seat," he said, voice low.

She gave him a crooked smile that didn't touch her eyes. "Usual's not doing it for me tonight."

His attention cut to the two empty glasses on her side, the fresh whiskey in front of her, then the untouched water. He didn't comment. Didn't reach for the glass. Just leaned forward, forearms braced on the table, steadying himself in her space. "Good thing I don't do usual either."

Sloane exhaled through her nose, like the weight of that sentence landed heavier than she'd expected. "After our conversation," she said softly, "I didn't know when expect to see you again."

Her eyes lifted, tired but daring. "You're back?"

Daniel leaned forward until the dim bar light caught the strong line of his jaw. "I'm back. I called you. Your phone is off."

She snorted, trying for careless, but her voice cracked on the edges. "Yours was off for days. Days, Daniel. Days I didn't know if you were alive or dead."

His gaze flicked to the silver chain twisting between her fingers, then returned to her face. "I'm sorry. Civilian comms blackout is part of the job. And I hated every minute I knew you'd worry."

Her throat tightened. She looked away—toward her bike, toward the streetlamp glow, toward anything that wasn't him. "I don't know if I can do this again."

Daniel's voice stayed steady, deeper now, the kind of tone that carried without rising. "I get that. But we both know risk doesn't negotiate. No day is promised."

He paused, gaze anchored on her face. "But you're not drinking because you're scared. Sloane... you're drinking because you want something. And pretending you don't terrifies you more than anything I face out there."

Her glass froze halfway to her lips. Her pulse thudded visibly at her throat.

Daniel didn't push. Didn't crowd. He just stayed—solid, unflinching, giving her the space to breathe or break.

She didn't breathe.

He flagged Sam with two fingers, never looking away from her. Sam wandered over, gave Daniel a nod that spoke volumes, and Daniel asked, "She eaten?"

Sam's look answered before he spoke. "Sliders," Daniel said. "Fried cheese. Two of each. Coffee for me. Coke for her."

Sloane glared at him, sharp enough to draw blood. "I didn't ask you to—"

"Didn't ask," he cut in gently. "That's why it'll work."

Sam set down the drinks first—Daniel's black coffee steaming, her Coke fizzing cold. "Diet," Sam chuckled. "So you have room for fries."

Sloane flipped him off without heat and threw back the rest of her whiskey like it was punishment.

Daniel wrapped both hands around his coffee mug, grounding himself. "Hydrate," he said, nodding toward her Coke. "Or I'll sit here all night and watch you glare at me. Your choice."

The Coke was half gone before the sliders hit the table. She tried not to look like she was devouring them, but the second bite left grease on her wrist and a sheepish smirk tugging at her mouth.

Daniel didn't gloat. He didn't need to. He just watched her with that quiet, steady patience—the kind that made her pulse slow for the first time in days.

"Better," he said, voice low.

She narrowed her eyes, wiping her fingers. "Bossy."

"When it matters," he countered.

Sam dropped the check, sliding it toward Daniel with a look that was half warning, half gratitude. Then he retreated, leaving them in the half-shadowed booth with nothing between them now but the truth they'd both been running from.

***

Sloane swallowed hard, suddenly aware of how close Daniel sat—his arm draped along the back of the booth, his knee brushing hers under the table, his presence a warm, steady weight pressing into the air between them. She glanced at the empty whiskey glass, at the untouched water, at him.

"You scared me," she whispered, the words so soft they barely disturbed the air.

Daniel's jaw flexed once—a controlled fracture. "I know," he said quietly. "And I'm here now."

Something in her chest loosened—just a thread.

She pulled her knees up slightly, curling toward herself. Daniel shifted almost imperceptibly, body angling as if ready to catch her if she tipped.

"Eat one more fry," he murmured. "Then we talk."

Her lips twitched. "You think you're in charge?"

He leaned in until the air between them warmed. "Sloane," he said, low and deliberate, "I know when someone's falling apart. And I'm not letting you do it alone."

Her breath stuttered. She didn't argue.

Chapter 6

B y the time she stood, Daniel was already on his feet, jacket in one hand, keys in the other. She glanced out the window at her bike, still gleaming under the streetlamp.

"Not tonight," he said—quiet, but absolute.

She opened her mouth, ready to argue, but he lifted the keys once, a small, unyielding command.

"Top down. Fresh air. I'll bring you back for it tomorrow."

The convertible's leather was cool against her thighs, the night air rushing over her as he pulled from the lot. It wasn't the sharp slap of whiskey anymore, but something gentler—wind in her hair, engine humming steady beneath them, Daniel beside her like gravity.

Her walls felt thinner here, stripped by motion and silence.

She leaned back, eyes closing for a moment—just long enough to forget why she'd tucked herself into a booth in the first place.

When she opened them, Daniel's profile was lit by passing street-lamps—jaw set, eyes on the road, his hand loose on the gearshift, close enough that she felt his heat with every shift.

The wind tugged at her hair as she traced a lazy line along the doorframe, watching the streetlights blur.

"Clear," she said finally.

Then she turned toward him, lips quirking. "And you've watched me for months."

His mouth twitched. "Ten."

"Fine. Ten." She shook her head, laughing under her breath.

"You know I never drive after one drink. The guys already planned to pick it up."

Daniel shifted gears, gaze still forward. "I know."

She angled toward him, brow raised. "So... where are we going? My house was three blocks back."

The road softened into gravel, then into a long, tree-lined drive. Pines arched above them, the headlights sweeping over a low, wide house tucked back from the road.

Not new. Not showy. A place for living, not performing.

Daniel eased the convertible to a stop, killed the engine, and let the night settle around them—crickets, the scent of pine, the faint rush of wind through dark branches.

Sloane looked at the house, then at him. "So... your place?"

"Yes."

His hands stayed loose on the wheel. "There are plenty of rooms. You can have your own if you want. We can go back to yours if you'd rather—but if we do, I'm staying."

He turned his head toward her, eyes steady, anchored. "The people in my life don't fight alone."

Her breath caught, sharper than she expected.

"So I'm in your life now?"

"Yes."

She swallowed, looking back at the house. "You're sure about this?"

Daniel reached for the keys, then paused, brow furrowing slightly. "I can turn around if you need anything from your place—meds, whatever. I should've asked earlier."

A shadow of a smile tugged his mouth. "Sorry. Got ahead of myself."

Her lips curved, crooked and real. "Yeah, you did."

She pushed the door open, boots hitting gravel. "But it's fine."

Daniel climbed out too, falling into step beside her. "Good."

It wasn't sterile, but it wasn't cluttered either. A house without pretense. Everything in its place. Everything serving a purpose. Everything quietly, unmistakably his.

Then she stepped into the living room and stopped.

Floor-to-ceiling built-ins lined one wall. Rows of spines, some worn smooth, others stiff and new.

Military histories. Survival manuals. Biographies. Classics.

But the far-left case pulled her in immediately—bright fantasy covers, dragons curled around sword hilts, vampires smoldering from glossy jackets, and wedged between them... a bodice-ripper featuring a half-dressed Highlander.

Her lips curved slow. "Never figured you for a teenage vampire fan."

Daniel glanced up as he set her bag on a chair, caught her expression, and exhaled through his nose. "I'm not."

She plucked a paperback from the shelf, turned it in her hand, and raised a brow. "Oh? So *Blood Kissed Shadows* just wandered in on its own?"

His mouth twitched—the closest thing to a laugh she'd seen from him. "I have a younger sister. Thinks she's hilarious sneaking things into my shelves."

Sloane slid the book back into place, smiling now. "And you just let her?"

Daniel shrugged, easy and unguarded. "She buys them at yard sales. I know she does it just to goad me. But... it makes her happy."

Sloane leaned against the shelf, arms folding across her chest, eyes softening despite herself.

The man who catalogued her Tuesday nights, who worried about porch lights, who carried himself like an iron-bound rule wrapped in calm—

had fantasy novels lined up beside tactical manuals because his little sister said so.

"Good to know you've got a weakness," she murmured, voice low, teasing.

Daniel stepped closer, just enough to erase the last inch of space between them.

"I do."

His eyes locked on hers, steady, knowing. "But it's not them."

***

She left the shelf, drifting farther into the room, and her eyes caught the corner.

A guitar rested there—wood worn smooth by years of hands, the strap looped in a lazy curve like it had been lifted and set down a hundred times.

Sloane hesitated, glancing at him.

Daniel gave the barest nod.

Permission.

Her fingers hovered over the strap, waiting for the hesitation that used to choke her—but it didn't come.

Daniel's nod was enough.

She slid the strap over her shoulder and settled the guitar against her body like it had never left her.

"I haven't held one in... gods. "A breathy laugh escaped her. "Over a decade, I guess."

Her hands remembered before her head did.

The first tentative strum buzzed sharp from strings slightly out of tune, but muscle memory took over.

Adjust. Shift. Find the chord.

Then—

She played.

A simple progression at first—slow, easy, the kind of melody you hum without realizing.

"Well, I started out walking with no clear road," she murmured, "just dust on my boots and too much time to think..."

Daniel leaned against the doorway, arms folded, watching the way her shoulders eased, the way her voice threaded through the quiet house like it belonged there.

She shifted into another line, softer, something half-written years ago:

"Learning to rise when the ground gives way, teaching myself how to breathe again..."

The last chord trembled as it faded. She let the guitar settle against her ribs and gave him a crooked smile.

"Guess some things stick."

Daniel's throat worked once.

"Yeah," he rasped. "The important ones do."

She slid the strap off and held the guitar out to him.

But instead of asking what he liked to play, her gaze flicked to the small black notebook he'd set on the shelf when they walked in.

"You ever play anything you write in there?" she asked softly.

Something shifted in him—not shock, but the quiet kind of surprise a man feels when someone notices more than he meant to show.

He took the guitar from her, hands careful.

"Yeah," he said. "I've been working on something since I landed."

Her breath caught. "Today?"

He nodded once, jaw tightening.

"There were things I should've said before I left."

He adjusted a tuning peg—a stalling motion—then let his fingers fall into a slow, grounded progression.

Not polished. Not perfect. Raw.

His voice followed, low and rough-edged:

"You moved a line I'd guarded for months ,and I left you standing there with nothing to hold. Felt that mistake the minute I landed—felt your silence harder than the dark."

A chord shift—deeper, aching.

"Time's a blade—I've lived by the edge. I won't cut you again by standing too far. As open as a man like me gets, I stand—bare, unguarded—and I'm sorry for the dark I caused you to fear."

The last note faded into the room like smoke.

Daniel lifted his head—

no shield, no grin, nothing to hide behind.

Just a man standing in front of her with his chest unarmored.

Sloane swallowed hard, breath catching in her ribcage.

He hadn't played a song.

He'd laid himself bare.

She stepped closer before she could think better of it, her hand brushing the neck of the guitar as she eased it from him and set it gently against the wall.

His eyes tracked her, warm, unreadable, and he didn't step back.

Not an inch.

"Funny thing about songs..." she murmured, her gaze rising to his. "...sometimes they say the shit we can't."

The space between them went electric.

***

She leaned in until her breath ghosted his jaw, body finally deciding what her head had been fighting for months. For half a heartbeat she braced to make the first move herself—always the one to leap, always the one to land alone.

But Daniel moved first.

Two fingers under her chin. A tilt. Quiet. Commanding.

His mouth found hers—deliberate from the opening stroke, no hesitation, no apology. Her pulse slammed once, hard, like it remembered every Tuesday night he'd watched her without touching.

She pressed forward. He let her—let it land—then shifted his weight, guiding her back until the wall met her spine, cool and solid behind the heat rolling off him.

He broke the kiss just enough to rasp against her lips, voice scraped raw. "That what you wanted?"

Her breath caught—jagged, honest. She nodded.

A slow, dangerous curve touched his mouth. "Good."

Then he kissed her again. Deeper. Hungrier. One hand braced beside her head, the other low at her hip—holding her exactly where she could feel every inch of what ten months of restraint had cost him.

He gave her a beat to feel it: eyes searching his, chest rising in uneven pulls, thighs already trembling against the press of him. Then his hand slid up, cupped beneath her chin—firm, unyielding—tilting her into the kiss he'd locked down for a goddamn year.

Precision. Pressure. Hunger. The kind that carved inside her ribs and lit it up slow.

Her body answered before her brain caught up—arching, pressing, nails finding his shoulders through cotton like she needed anchors. By the time she registered the shift, she was flush to the wall, Daniel a heated cage in front of her, solid as iron, patient as fire waiting for wind.

His mouth dragged to her cheek, voice gravel dragged over silk. "Sloane. Look at me."

She did. The house dissolved. Just his eyes—dark, steady, unflinching—and the weight of him pinning her like gravity finally had permission to pull.

"If you need me to stop," he said, thumb tracing her jaw, grounding even as he held her captive, "say it."

She swallowed. Voice barely there. "I'd tell you."

A flicker of smile—sharp, relieved. "Good. I don't guess."

Then his mouth claimed hers again—harder, hotter— fingers threading into her hair, anchoring her head, other hand gripping her hip with the quiet strength she'd felt in every glance he'd never let linger too long.

He kissed her like restraint was a rope he'd finally cut. Like she was the air he'd been holding his breath against.

His grip shifted—lower, bolder—fingers catching the curve of her thigh. One smooth lift. Her leg hooked around his hip like it belonged there.

She gasped into his mouth, nails biting deeper. This was the man she'd imagined in the dark: controlled, lethal in his want, and now every ounce of that control was locked on her.

He dragged his mouth down her jaw, her neck—teeth grazing just enough to promise more. "You've been testing me for ten months," he growled, voice frayed at the edges. "This is what you were asking for."

Her head tipped back, body curving into him on instinct. "Maybe."

"Not maybe." Teeth at her throat—restraint fraying thread by thread.

The wall held. Daniel held harder. And for once he let her feel the full weight of him—no distance, no mask, just heat and certainty and the promise he wasn't letting her slip away tonight.

Her confession slipped out, raw, unbidden. "Daniel... it's been over a year. I haven't—"

His hand left her hair. Thumb brushed her lips—quiet command. "Shhh."

Eyes locked on hers again—dark, sure, steady. "I know."

That thumb dragged slow across her lower lip, melting her knees even pinned. "We go at your pace. Slow or fast. You call it."

His next breath brushed her cheek—shaking with everything he was caging. "But damn it, woman... you need to feel—for one god-damn minute—the fire you started."

Her fingers curled tight in his shirt. "I want to."

The sound he made was half growl, half surrender. He kissed her again—deeper, claiming— lifted her other leg until her thighs locked around his waist, body caged between wall and heat.

Restraint held. Barely.

He broke away just enough to murmur against her ear, words vibrating through bone. "Tell me when you want me to stop."

Her answer wasn't words—just a low, needy sound. More plea than permission.

"Good," he rasped, teeth finding her neck again. "Then hold on."

For the first time in a year, she did. Body to body. Fire for fire. Letting herself burn exactly the way she'd been starving to.

He lowered her slow—boots finding floor, hands lingering at her hips like letting go was still negotiable. Her eyes flicked away for one second.

That was all he needed.

He swept her up without warning—arms under her thighs, back supported, carrying her like he'd earned the right months ago.

Her gasp cracked the quiet. "Why—"

"Because I can." Low. Absolute. Final.

He carried her through the back door like the night belonged to them both.

***

The night air bit cooler here, stars scattered sharp overhead, steam curling from the hot tub tucked in the deck's corner. Daniel set her down in front of it—close enough to feel the heat rising, close enough the air between them tightened like wire.

The backyard stretched wide under the stars—amber sconces in stonework, outdoor kitchen built for quiet nights, long dark lap pool still as glass. Sloane's breath eased, a slow inhale she hadn't known she was holding. Daniel watched her take it in, hands warm at her waist, forearms taut but unhurried.

"Strip," he said, voice low, command wrapped in gravel. "Or I'll do it for you."

Her lips curved, daring. "You first."

His mouth kicked wolfish. Shirt peeled off, belt pulled slow and deliberate. Boots, jeans—gone in seconds. He stood shameless in the water-glow, scars pale brushstrokes across muscle. Nothing hidden. Nothing softened. Just Daniel—solid, unapologetic, built for function and heat.

"Your turn." He stepped closer, steam blurring the line, gaze heavy as touch.

Sloane's pulse kicked. Chin lifted anyway. Boots unlaced slow, set neat side-by-side. Socks. Bare feet on cool wood. Shirt off in one motion. Black bra, simple, functional—no lace, no frills. Button fly popped loud in the quiet. Denim slid, pooled. Panties matched: black, no apology.

"I like simple," she said, folding her arms across ribs. "Get-the-job-done clothes."

Daniel's eyes traced her—deliberately—memorizing, not consuming. "Good." Voice rough. "Because I'm not here for lace." He stepped into her. Hand brushed her hip—firm, steady, claiming her shape like he'd waited long enough. "I'm here for you."

Her breath caught. Arms crossed tighter, instinctive brace—but his gaze stripped it anyway.

"See something you like?"

His gaze never wavered—dark, unhurried. "Everything." Fingers flexed on her hip. "And none of it's simple."

She snorted, soft. "Liar. Black cotton isn't exactly a seduction."

He leaned in—close enough his breath brushed her ear. "It is when it's on you."

Her pulse kicked hard. Arms loosened.

She stepped down. Heat curled up her legs. Inch by inch she sank deeper, the ache in every joint beginning to uncoil. Shoulders rolled back, eyes fluttered shut, a sigh slipped free—low, unguarded, intimate. Steam kissed her skin, dampened her hair. For the first time in too long, she let herself feel.

Daniel watched from the edge. She felt the impact of it in the way his attention locked on her, heavy and unmoving. Only when her eyes opened did he slide in. Water hissed around his thighs, steam swirling hard lines.

He circled once—slow, predatory—claiming the space, giving her time to feel him before touch. Sloane tipped her head back against stone, lips parted, body open in a way she hadn't meant to allow.

He came up behind her—chest heat meeting water heat. Hands slid under the surface, found her waist. Strong. Steady. Guiding her back against him.

"You're always braced," he rasped at her ear. "Even now. Even here." Thumbs stroked arcs over hips. "Breathe. Let it go."

Then he turned her—deliberate—until she faced him, thighs bracketing his on the ledge, water lapping just below her breasts.

"Look at me," he murmured.

She did—over steam, over heat, breath thick and shared. He dipped his head, brushed lips over temple... cheek... edge of mouth—teasing, waiting. She leaned in. Their lips met, slow at first, then deeper when she pressed back into him. The kiss stole her breath, gave it back warm—tasting of want and months of held restraint.

"That's it," he whispered against her lips. "Stay with me."

Hand slid lower through water, tracing thigh in slow circles, learning her breath's rhythm. But his mouth kept returning—jaw, cheek, mouth again and again—steadying her with lips as much as hands.

Sloane gasped into the kiss when he found her. Fingers clutched his thigh beneath water—not balance, connection. Daniel groaned soft, the sound vibrating through her.

Her head fell back; he caught her chin, turned her into another kiss—deeper, needier—pulling a helpless sound from her throat. He broke only to breathe against her mouth. "Sloane... I'm right here."

Strokes matched her stutter—thighs tensing, chest rising broken, lips trembling as he kissed her through every shift. "Eyes on me."

She tried. When her gaze faltered, he kissed her again, guiding her back with his mouth, thumb brushing cheek. "Let go. With me."

"Do you feel it?" Rough whisper. "That's me wanting you." "I'll go as slow as you need... or take you apart inch by inch." "But you're not basic. And you're not alone."

"Safe," he murmured. "You're safe with me. Say it."

Head tipped back, steam rising, lips parting— "Safe," she gasped.

The word cracked her open. Thighs tightened against his wrist. Release built fast—heat rising, breath breaking, hips trembling. Her cry muffled against his mouth as it hit—wave after wave from her core outward, body shuddering against him. Voice broke on his name.

Daniel held her—hand steady between thighs, arm tight across ribs, mouth brushing cheek in grounding strokes. He kissed her through every tremor—mouth, jaw, corner of lips—anchoring her until she slumped boneless against his chest, dazed.

When breathing steadied, he kissed the corner of her mouth—slow, tender, reverent. "Yeah," he whispered. "I felt you."

And she felt him—the want, the restraint pulled thin, the connection threading their breaths, the way her pleasure echoed through him too.

He gathered her up without a word. Lifted her easy from the water. Limbs trembled—not fear, but everything carried too long, finally set down. Everything she'd finally let go.

***

She would push herself until she broke; she could feel him reading it in every line of her body.

He scooped her up, water streaming down her skin, her head falling heavy against his shoulder. She made a soft protest—almost a laugh.

"I can walk."

"You don't need to. "His tone invited no argument. "Not tonight."

He carried her to the deck and set her gently on the wide lounger. The night air touched her damp skin, raising gooseflesh, and before the shiver settled he wrapped a towel around her—tucking it snug, shielding her like he meant it.

He crossed to the outdoor fridge, grabbed two chilled water bottles, cracked one open, and pressed it into her hand.

"Drink."

Her lips curved, teasingly. "Bossy."

Daniel gave a single slow nod against her temple—yes, deal with it—then slid in behind her on the lounger, legs bracketing her hips, chest warm against her back.

She stilled—just for a breath—then leaned into him, letting her weight settle against his body. He wrapped one arm around her, rubbing slow circles along her upper arm with the other, grounding her with touch alone.

He pressed a warm, barely-there kiss to the crown of her damp hair.

Above them, the sky stretched wide—velvet, scattered with stars. "The Little Dipper," she whispered suddenly, pointing upward. "I haven't looked in forever."

Daniel followed her line. "There. And Orion—see the belt?"

She nodded, voice drifting softer with each constellation they traded. Not experts—just two people remembering fragments of childhood and handing them to each other under the night sky.

Her breathing slowed, her body settling deeper into him as the minutes stretched. She tipped her head toward him again, half-laughing, half-asleep.

When she finished the water, he took the bottle from her fingers and shifted his hold, drawing the towel a little tighter around her before guiding her knees over his thighs.

She resisted for a heartbeat—reflex—then her body surrendered, curling into his chest like she'd finally found a place that could hold her weight.

Steam thinned in the night air. Daniel's arms stayed around her—loose but sure. Her head tucked naturally against his shoulder, her breath warming the skin just above his collarbone.

"That one's easy," she murmured, pointing again with a lazy flick. "The Big Dipper."

Daniel followed her gesture "And Cassiopeia. My father used to trace it for my sister when she couldn't sleep."

She hummed, soft. "We camped in the Appalachians once. I always thought Orion's belt looked like sparks."

His smile warmed against her hair. "Still does."

Their words drifted in and out of the night—comfortable, quiet—fragments of memory glowing between them like lantern light.

Her body grew heavier by degrees, muscles slackening, breath evening out. Her fingers slipped from the empty bottle, falling to rest against his forearm. A soft, involuntary sigh left her parted lips.

Daniel didn't move. Her weight settled fully into him, the guarded lines of her frame loosening at last.

Her body grew heavy against his, breath deepening, edges of the night blurring as sleep took her. The peace settled in, deep and undeniable.

They stayed there under the stars until the night cooled and her breathing deepened, the rhythm of her pressed to his chest.

Eventually, careful as breath, he shifted to stand. She stirred, murmured something soft and dream-heavy, then settled again, trusting him completely.

He let them feel one more quiet beat.

Then he rose, lifting her into his arms like nothing in the world could pull her from them now.

Chapter 7

Her body curled instinctively against his chest as he lifted her, one arm under her knees, the other steady along her back. She didn't protest. Didn't stir. Just a soft sigh, her head tucked into the warm crook of his neck.

Inside, the house was cool and still. Daniel nudged the bathroom door open with his shoulder, caught a towel from the shelf, and sat her gently on the edge of the counter.

Her eyes fluttered open—hazy, half-asleep, trusting.

"Just me," he murmured, running the towel through her damp hair. His touch was firm but careful, blotting, smoothing, taming the dripping strands like he'd done it a hundred times.

She tried to lift a hand—habit, independence—but he caught her wrist lightly and lowered it back to her lap.

"Indulge me."

Her eyelids dipped again, her breathing slowing.

When her head began to loll, he swept her back into his arms, the towel draped loosely over her shoulders. He carried her into the bedroom, the shadows soft, the sheets cool and waiting.

Daniel eased her onto the edge of the bed and tugged the towel free. She stirred faintly, lashes fluttering.

"Mmm...?"

"Shhh." His voice was steady, low, made of warmth and command.

He hooked his fingers into the waistband of her soaked cotton and slid it down her hips—slow, efficient, intimate. She made no protest, only shifted enough to let him, her breath soft and unguarded.

For a quiet moment he looked at her—bare, relaxed, open in a way she didn't give freely. Something deep in his chest pulled taut.

He crossed to his dresser, pulled out a soft worn T-shirt, the fabric carrying the faint scent of cedar and soap. He slipped it over her head, guided her arms through, tugged it down.

Sloane sighed—bone-deep, content—and sank into the sheets like her body recognized the difference instantly.

Daniel killed the light, slid into bed behind her, and pulled her against him—chest to her back, leg hooked against hers, one arm heavy at her waist.

She melted there, deeper than she'd yielded all night, her breath evening out before he'd even settled.

He buried his face against her damp hair and exhaled into the quiet.

She slept with his arm locked around her, breath warm against her neck, the steady weight of him anchoring her through the dark.

***

The first blush of dawn spilled through wide panes of glass, painting the hardwood in pale gold. No curtains. No blinds. Just raw light cutting across the room.

Sloane groaned, burrowing deeper under the sheets. Warm cotton tangled around her legs, but it couldn't shield her from the sun pricking at her eyelids.

A heavy arm anchored her at the waist. Daniel—half awake but steady—shifted behind her, the heat of his chest pressed along her back. His breathing was slow, unhurried, the kind that came easy to a man used to rising with the sun.

She shoved the covers over her head.

"Gods. It's inhumane. No curtains?"

Daniel's chest rumbled with a low laugh. He pressed a kiss to the top of her head, his voice still rough with sleep.

"I like waking with the sun."

"Inhumane," she repeated, louder now—but the edge softened when she rolled onto her back to look at him.

His eyes were already open. Still dark. Still focused entirely on her.

And then the memories hit—steam rising around her skin, his hands steady under water his mouth at her throat, his voice coaxing her open until her body broke apart in his arms.

Heat swept through her beneath the thin T-shirt he'd pulled onto her last night.

He'd given her everything... and hadn't taken anything for himself.

Unfair. Unbalanced. And she hated uneven.

"Blackout curtains are better," she decided, tossing the sheets off and swinging one leg over him, straddling his hips. Her hair spilled over her shoulders, eyes narrowing in challenge. "But for now? It's your turn."

Daniel lay still beneath her, gaze steady as he watched her—calm, composed, wolfish.

"My turn," he confirmed, his voice a low rasp.

"That's right."

He let her settle. Let her lean in. Let her think she'd claimed the lead.

Then his fingers wrapped around her wrists—firm, controlled—and he gave a sharp swat to the curve of her ass.

The sound cracked through the sunlit room.

She gasped—more surprise than pain—her body jolting against him.

Before she could recover, he rolled her beneath him in one smooth motion, guiding her wrists above her head, her back sinking into the mattress.

A slow, wicked smile curved her mouth.

"Your turn," she teased, breathless already.

Daniel held her wrists high, strength humming beneath his restraint. Her chest lifted with each quick breath, her body already answering him.

His mouth dropped to hers in a kiss that landed hard—hungry, deliberate—his tongue stroking hers until her back arched into him.

When he broke the kiss, his breath scraped hot against her lips.

"You really thought you had control this morning?"

"Maybe," she whispered, though her pulse betrayed her.

His smirk darkened.

"Not today."

He reached for the nightstand. She followed the motion, eyes darkening as he tore the foil with his teeth, his free hand already sliding lower.

He sheathed himself with practiced ease, his gaze never leaving hers.

When he came back over her, settling his weight between her thighs, her legs opened without hesitation—like her body remembered him from the night before.

He recaptured her wrists, pinning them above her head, her breath catching as she yielded beneath him.

He paused at her entrance—a single, deliberate heartbeat of heat and tension.

Sloane bit her lip and nodded once.

He pushed in slowly, inch by inch, watching her face as she stretched around him—her mouth falling open on a gasp, her hips tilting to take him deeper.

The sound she made tore free.

Daniel swallowed it with a kiss, driving deeper.

"I'm not fragile," she whispered, fierce even now.

His grip tightened, anchoring her.

"Good," he growled. "Then hold on."

She did.

Her hips rose to meet every thrust, sunlight spilling across tangled sheets as he drove her higher—answering every arch of her spine, every tremor, every breathless sound.

He coaxed her open all over again—mouth, hands, rhythm—until she shattered beneath him, once, then again, crying his name into his mouth.

Only then did he follow, control finally breaking as his body shook with hers—raw, unguarded, and fully claimed.

***

Her body was still trembling when he eased back, his breath rough against her hair.

He didn't let her drift. Didn't let her curl away.

He slid an arm beneath her shoulders, another under her knees, and lifted her clean off the mattress.

"Daniel—"

"Shower," he said—iron and smoke. "We're not finished."

The water was already hot by the time he stepped them in. Steam curled around them, plastering her hair to her shoulders, running in rivulets down the curve of her spine.

He braced her against the tile, hands firm at her hips. The cascade beat down her back while his mouth traced the line of her throat—slow, claiming drags of teeth and tongue that made her knees go weak.

"You needed last night," he rasped against her jaw. "Needed release. Safety."

His breath scraped hot along her ear.

"Needed to remember you still belong to your own skin."

Her gasp caught when his hand slipped between them—sure, demanding—finding her already slick and open. Heat shot through her, her hips tipping instinctively into his touch.

And then he pushed into her in one sharp thrust.

Her breath broke as the wall met her back, her body opening around him without hesitation.

"This," he growled against her neck, his hips driving deep again, "is what I've been holding back."

The shower drowned her moans.

Water slid over her skin as her palms slapped against the glass for balance. Daniel's hand tangled in her wet hair, pulling her head back to bare her throat—exposing every inch he wanted.

His teeth grazed her pulse.

She shook all over.

"Hold on," he ordered, voice low, thick.

He changed the angle—lifted her higher—and she broke.

Her climax hit so hard her legs locked around his waist, her entire body clenching around him.

He thrust through it, pulling a second cry from her throat, holding her pinned between his body and the tile like she was the only thing anchoring him.

He chased his own release with single-minded hunger she felt in every snap of his hips.

When it tore through him, he groaned into her neck—raw, guttural—his body shuddering with hers as the water washed them clean.

For a long moment, he didn't move.

Just held her there, her back against the tile, his chest heaving against hers.

Then—without a word—he shut off the water and lifted her again, carrying her from the tub.

She didn't even try to stand. Her body was boneless in his arms.

He wrapped her in a towel, swaddling her tight, then pressed a soft kiss to her temple—so gentle it almost hurt.

"Still think blackout curtains are your biggest problem?" he murmured.

She laughed—wrecked, breathless. "One of them."

He blotted her hair with quiet precision, fingers threading through damp strands like he needed the contact to settle himself.

Then a sharp, playful swat to her backside snapped the air.

"Top drawer," he said, his voice still hoarse from her name in his throat. "Grab something if you want."

Sloane blinked, dazed. Nodded.

Clothes .Coffee. Reality. Right.

"Coffee?" he called over his shoulder as he walked out, towel low on his hips.

"Gods, yes," she managed, her voice raw around the edges.

He disappeared down the hall.

She stood there a beat too long, fingers brushing the drawer pull—still trembling, still breath-short, still trying to remember which planet she was on.

***

Daniel slung a second towel low around his hips and stepped onto the deck, the morning air cold against his skin.

Their clothes were scattered where he'd dropped them last night—his shirt ,her jeans, her bra a dark coil near the spa, her boots tipped on their sides.

He crouched, gathering each piece, fingers brushing over worn denim and soft cotton still warm from the earlier heat between them. A quiet exhale left him—half laugh, half disbelief.

He hadn't expected the night to go the way it had. Hadn't expected the morning to hit harder.

Sloane had curled into him with a trust that lodged under his ribs. A trust she didn't give easily. A trust he'd nearly broken once already by disappearing without warning.

That thought landed heavy.

He straightened, her jeans draped over his arm, and made a silent vow—he'd find a way to reassure her next time he was gone. A channel that wasn't personal, but dependable. A number his employees' families used, a line he'd never needed...until now.

He stepped back inside, the warmth of the house wrapping around him.

The kitchen was dim, morning soft through the windows. He set her clothes gently on the counter, started the kettle, then the coffee—her coffee.

Sloane would walk out soon—damp hair, sore legs, T-shirt swallowing her frame, pretending she wasn't still trembling.

She'd call him bossy. Steal half his breakfast. Act like she hadn't just come apart in his hands twice this morning.

His mouth pulled into a slow, private grin.

She had no idea how deep she'd sunk into him already. And he wasn't planning on giving that space back.

***

By the time she padded into the kitchen in one of his soft, oversized shirts, Daniel was already at the counter—bare-chested, coffee steaming, eggs cracking into a pan like the world hadn't tilted sideways an hour ago.

She leaned against the doorway, watching him move.

Steady. Capable.

No hesitation in his hands—just rhythm.

Like he already knew what she needed before she said a word.

"I've been curious about those cooking skills you mentioned," she said, her voice softer than before.

He looked over his shoulder, mouth curving.

"Just basics this morning. Don't expect a soufflé."

She smiled.

Good.

Smirking was safer than silence.

"You mentioned your sister last night," she said, sliding onto a stool. "You two close?"

He set a plate in front of her, coffee beside it.

"Yeah. She's younger. Mouthier. Reminds me of you, actually."

She lifted her cup.

"Poor woman."

He grinned.

"She'd say the same."

He sat beside her, thigh against hers—the warmth of him easy, deliberate. Nothing loud. Nothing rushed. Just presence.

He took a bite of toast.

"You have other siblings besides a sister with minimal music variety?"

She sipped her coffee before answering.

"An older brother. He's a pharmacist."

A crooked smirk.

"He's the practical one of the bunch."

Daniel chuckled, shaking his head.

"Parents still together?"

She raised a brow.

"Yeah. Weird, right? Married thirty-eight years. Still holding hands in parking lots."

"Jesus."

He lifted his coffee.

"That's not normal."

"Nope. Five-percent anomaly. Romantic stability—absolutely disgusting."

He smiled, but something thoughtful flickered beneath it.

"You close with them?"

"Close enough."

A beat.

"They mean well. Don't always know what to do with me, but... they try."

She nudged her cup aside, studying him.

"What about yours?"

His hands stilled briefly on the rim of his mug.

"Dad's still around. Mom passed when I was twenty."

His voice softened—not heavy. Just honest.

"Dad worked double shifts to cover her care. I handled most things with my sister."

Sloane blinked, something warm and quiet settling behind her eyes.

"Your sister's the one who sneaks the vampire books onto your shelves?"

He huffed a low laugh.

"Yeah. Little menace. Thinks she's teaching me something."

"She might be right."

"Don't encourage her."

Sloane laughed—a small, genuine sound that eased something in his chest.

They ate in a quiet that wasn't strained. Wasn't heavy.

Settled. Easy.

Two people letting their worlds overlap without force.

Later, in the car, the silence held the same shape.

Sun caught in her hair as she watched the town pass by, one leg curled beneath his sweatshirt where it swallowed her thighs.

Her eyes were softer now. Her body still warm from his bed. The air between them less charged—but no less tethered.

She wasn't retreating.

Just processing.

Letting herself feel the morning in pieces, the way he did.

Daniel glanced over once—just long enough to catch the corner of her mouth soften before she turned back to the window.

It did something quiet to him.

He kept driving.

Kept the silence intact.

Some moments didn't need filling.

***

His thumb brushed absently against the inside of her wrist as he turned onto her street, right where her pulse still jumped for him.

"You're still thinking about it," she said, catching the tell.

He glanced at her.

She tilted her head, eyes playful but unreadable.

"Was the appointment a ploy to see me again," she asked, "or are you actually ready to trust me with something permanent?"

"Both," he said, unapologetic.

Her smile curved—slow, deliberate.

"Well, if you've changed your mind," she said lightly, "now's your chance."

"I stand by my decisions."

His voice was solid. Anchored. Certain.

She opened the door, half out before glancing back.

"Something else we have in common."

He cocked a brow.

"You gonna show me the design?"

"Nope."

She flashed a grin, all heat and challenge.

"You'll see it when the needle hits skin."

Something in his expression shifted—resolve settling in.

His mouth found hers in a kiss that felt claimed and chosen at the same time. Slow. Certain. Grounding.

When he pulled back, his thumb lingered at her jaw like a signature.

She smiled once more—softer this time—then slipped out of the car.

He waited until the door clicked shut.

Daniel sat there a moment longer, the place she'd left still warm.

The kiss replayed—not the heat of it, but the way it had settled him.

How easy it felt to choose restraint instead of distance. How right it felt to let her walk away knowing she would come back.

Permanent didn't scare him. Trust didn't either.

He pulled away from the curb with a slow smile, already aware of the quiet truth taking shape in his chest—

This wasn't a risk.

It was a decision.

Sloane leaned back against the door once she was inside, breath finally leaving her in a shaky laugh.

Her mouth still tingled. Her pulse still carried his imprint.

She hadn't given him the design. Hadn't shown him the ink.

And he'd stayed anyway.

That mattered more than the night. More than the sex. More than the promise hovering between them.

She pushed off the door, already smiling to herself.

Some things were worth trusting.

Some men were worth marking.

Epilogue

D aniel didn't bother brushing the dirt off his boots when he
stepped inside.

It had been another long mission—one of the last he'd agreed to
take—and the drive back had carved exhaustion deep into his bones.

He expected silence.

Instead, the house glowed.

The small lamp he never touched was on. A blanket draped over the
back of the couch.

And curled into the far corner, legs tucked beneath her, was
Sloane—glasses perched low on her nose, hair an unapologetic
mess, Vizzini sprawled across her lap like a tiny tyrant.

She looked up slowly, a smirk blooming the moment she saw him.

"Hey," she said. "Your furry son's been yelling at me all night."

As if summoned, the kitten chirped and burrowed deeper into her
sweater.

Daniel dropped his duffel with a grunt.

For the first time in years—hell, decades—walking through a door
felt like stepping somewhere he actually belonged.

"You're reading that?" he asked, nodding at the paperback in her
hands.

Sloane lifted it. *The Princess Bride.*

The very book his sister had wedged into his romance shelf with zero shame.

"I figured if I'm kitten-sitting," she said dryly, "I'd finish the movie we started—with the book. You know. Understand your taste in... literature."

Daniel huffed a tired laugh.

"I never said I liked it."

"You didn't have to." She tapped the cover. "This explains so much."

He crossed the living room in three slow strides.

Sloane closed the book, marking her place with the corner of a takeout menu, and held out her free hand.

Daniel took it.

She rose, the blanket sliding from her legs, and the moment her body touched his, something in him unclenched.

He kissed her—not rushed, not hungry—just a long, steady exhale of a man finally home.

Sloane sighed against his mouth.

"Welcome back," she murmured.

"Missed you," he admitted, voice rough.

She brushed her thumb over the grime on his jaw.

"You look wrecked."

"Feel wrecked."

"You want food? Shower? Bed?"

"Just you," he said.

Not a line.

Truth.

Vizzini chose that moment to latch onto Daniel's boot, claws determined.

Sloane snorted.

"He's obsessed. I don't know what you did to him."

"Same thing I did to you," Daniel said.

"Showed up."

Her breath caught—just for a second.

He lowered his forehead to hers, thumb sweeping her cheekbone.

"No more vanishing," he murmured."I've wrapped up the last of the field work. You'll always have a line to me now."

She searched his face for hesitation.Found none.

"You're sure?" she whispered.

"I'm sure."

A long, warm silence settled between them.

Then Sloane nudged him lightly.

"Good. Because I was halfway through this book and needed you to explain why the fencing scenes feel like your autobiography."

Daniel groaned.

"Please don't tell my sister you said that."

"Oh, I'm absolutely telling her."

He kissed her again—laughing into her mouth this time.

She pushed him toward the hallway.

"Go shower before you fall over. I'll be here. Guarding your tiny menace."

He paused in the doorway, hand braced on the frame.

Sloane had already curled back into the couch, kitten draped across her legs, paperback open again.

And god help him—the sight made something quiet and permanent settle in his chest.

"Hey, Sloane?"

She looked up.

A slow smile tugged at his mouth.

"Feels good coming home to you."

Her smirk softened—just a little.

"Yeah," she said. "Feels good being here."

Daniel disappeared down the hall.

The shower kicked on.

Sloane flipped to the next page, blanket drawn over her lap, Vizzini purring like a motor beside her.

And the house—his house—felt warm, lived-in, and no longer empty.

About the author

Vaela Quinn writes from instinct rather than outline—stories born in the body before they ever reach the page. Her work is emotionally grounded and unapologetically intimate, exploring grief, desire, resilience, and connection with a precision that feels lived-in rather than imagined.

She doesn't write trauma as spectacle or romance as fantasy. She writes emotional reality—what it costs to survive, what it takes to trust again, and how intimacy grows in the quiet spaces where fear and want collide. Her characters aren't polished archetypes; they carry ghosts, habits, sharp edges, and hearts that learn how to open without breaking.

Vaela's storytelling is rooted in deep empathy and an unusual ability to step fully into another emotional landscape. She takes raw feeling and transmutes it into narrative with intention, crafting stories that don't just entertain, but *register*. Her heat is deliberate and earned, inseparable from character, and vulnerability is treated as strength rather than spectacle.

Vaela Quinn writes for readers who want to be **moved**, not soothed—
for those who recognize themselves in complicated longing, quiet courage, and the choice to begin again.

Also by

Also in the Small Town Bar Series

More stories set around Rosemary's are on the way.

Each book can be read on its own, connected by a bar where nights linger, conversations matter, and attraction has a habit of showing up uninvited.

Coming soon:

On the Rocks

A long-simmering connection, unfinished business, and the pull of a past that never quite let go.

Sangria & Sunsets

An architect. An artist. A meeting that turns reclaimed history into something neither of them expected.

Hot Toddy Elixir

A wedding week, a stubborn cold, and a remedy that works better than planned.

Mimosa Mornings

Sunlight, second chances, and the kind of morning-after that changes everything.